He shook his head. "I wanted to continue our conversation from last night."

"I get it. Your boss isn't interested." She fiddled with her table setting, the decorative plate turned clockwise, the cutlery brushed by her fingertips, but she watched him the whole while. "You might not have said the words, but they were obvious. There aren't any hard feelings."

"I spoke hastily," he said, continuing when she cocked her head with interest. "There is a project that could use your unique creations. Your vase tells a story, and I'd like to hear more of it." He'd reevaluated after observing her vase and seeing a beauty in it that he hadn't immediately recognized—after realizing that he couldn't allow her attractive qualities to blind him to a business opportunity with her.

"Are *you* offering the job or is your boss?"

Besides wanting to avoid the magnetic attraction he felt for her, this was the other reason he hadn't wanted to do this. Explaining that he, in fact, was the boss. Not for the first time, Karl regretted not speaking up sooner and clearing up the misunderstanding. *Too late for that now.*

With a hardened jaw, he said, "The shortest answer would be yes...to both."

Dear Reader,

For me, the holidays have always been about family gatherings, an excuse to eat a lot of delicious food, a break from work or school and community spirit.

The holidays are also a reset period for me. Though I don't make New Year's resolutions for myself anymore, I try to remember to both learn from and let go of the past—especially past mistakes.

In *Forbidden Kisses with Her Millionaire Boss*, Karl struggles to do just that, and he carries around this massive chip on his shoulder that makes him come off frosty and unapproachable to others. He has very few happy family memories, and the holidays aren't the cheeriest of times for him. That changes when Lin comes from Kenya to his home in Canada to work alongside him. Together, they hope to pull off a special event for his godmother. Unexpectedly, Lin also thaws the ice around his guarded heart.

Neither of them is bargaining to share anything more than a few forbidden kisses and a holiday fling, but what happens when their hearts aren't checking out after the holidays end?

I hope you enjoy reading Lin and Karl's story.

Happiest holidays,

Hana

Forbidden Kisses with Her Millionaire Boss

Hana Sheik

Recycling programs
for this product may
not exist in your area.

ISBN-13: 978-1-335-73691-8

Forbidden Kisses with Her Millionaire Boss

Harlequin Enterprises ULC
22 Adelaide St. West, 41st Floor
Toronto, Ontario M5H 4E3, Canada
www.Harlequin.com

Printed in U.S.A.

Hana Sheik falls in love every day reading her favorite romances and writing her own happily-ever-afters. She's worked various jobs—but never for very long because she's always wanted to be a romance author. Now she gets to happily live that dream. Born in Somalia, she moved to Ottawa, Canada, at a very young age, and still resides there with her family.

Books by Hana Sheik

Harlequin Romance

Second Chance to Wear His Ring
Temptation in Istanbul

Visit the Author Profile page at Harlequin.com.

This one is for all the holidays.

Thanks for the good food and cheering us up.

Praise for
Hana Sheik

CHAPTER ONE

Snow in Africa.

Karl Sinclair had thought he'd seen it all. Sky-diving nuptials, twelve-foot cakes suspended in midair and a holographic groomsman who couldn't make it to his brother's wedding on time. Nothing extravagant fazed him now.

And yet he froze at the crunch of snow beneath his patent leather sneakers.

The venue was as it should be. A luxury chalet constructed in two months and on schedule. Only instead of the cold climes being outdoors, the wintry theme had been brought inside. Just as he'd envisioned it when his clients approached him with ideas for their big day. Like all his previous events, the venue had come to life the way he knew it would. He never doubted his ability to reproduce the elaborate, memorable occasions his clients expected of his event-management company, Heartbeat Events. Karl hadn't thought he would travel from Canada to Nairobi, Kenya, to see it in person, though. With it being the middle of September, and nearer to the busy holiday season, he'd had one of his top event coordinators, Nadine, take over the project. At least, he had planned for it to be like that. Usually, his plans were foolproof once set on their course.

Only, he hadn't expected Nadine would come down with the flu at the very last moment.

Sending someone else in his place felt wrong. His clients expected a personal touch. *His* touch. And with the sky-high price tag on his service, the least he could do was carry the torch to the finish line. A line that would be crossed tomorrow once the bride and groom exchanged their vows and celebrated their reception with four hundred of their family and closest friends in this lavish venue.

The snow flooded the corridor like fluffy white clouds that had fallen from above. Karl turned his head up to admire the force of the air-conditioning. He stored a mental note to ensure that the building's management team monitored the HVAC system. The last thing anyone needed was costly damage to one of the compressors or refrigerants. Snow inside a Swiss chalet was romantic. Melted snow was another thing. His bride and groom hadn't signed up for an underwater reception. It was his job to coordinate everything and see that the snow remained in its solid state.

He popped up the collar of his overcoat, glad he'd remembered to dress appropriately for his tour.

The snow followed him from the chalet's entrance up a winding flight of stairs to the mezzanine overlooking the main hall. Spanning five thousand square feet, the hall's jet-black floors were covered with sixty-three tables seating eight each, according to the notes from Nadine's detailed report. Security would see to it that no extra plus-ones slipped into the private event. No one crashed his parties. Exclusivity was part of his brand. High-profile clients paid for their privacy as much as the glamour, glitz and romance.

Buttoning his coat, Karl tensed his muscles against the shiver skittering up and down his spine. Once again, he was relieved to have chosen attire that withstood the frigid blast of the building's top-notch air-conditioning.

It was also how he knew that the woman striding up the striking white aisle runner down below wasn't where she ought to be.

Her endlessly long dark brown legs were what caught his attention first. Easy to admire that part of her when she wore a miniskirt. The striped skirt suited her long-sleeved wrap crop top, as did her red-soled Louboutin pumps. She hadn't noticed him watching from above. She walked purposefully down the aisle created for the central moment when the newlyweds joined their guests at the reception and climbed the short set of steps to the wedding-party table. The table was set with florid centerpieces. Gold candelabra with pearl-encrusted handles, exquisite Wedgwood tableware and gold-wire vases he could only describe as unique in design. They were empty now, but tomorrow they would be brimming with frost-resistant floral arrangements: camellias, winterberries, evergreen sprigs and a few other hardy perennials he couldn't recall from Nadine's report. And he wasn't making a real effort to remember.

The woman down below had his full attention.

She carried a vase that she set down on the table. Then plucking up an identical one, she eyed it shrewdly, turning it this way and that, her chin-length sleek black bob swinging briskly with her movements. Seemingly having made a decision, she traded the one vase for the other.

What's she up to?

He narrowed his eyes and gripped the railing, his jaw full of unyielding steel and his curiosity overriding the goal to survey the venue for any minute missing details. Keyed up, he stalked toward the stairs. Taking them two at a time, he reached the ground floor and headed to intercept the mystery woman.

She gasped when he was halfway to her, her body going rigid, hands stilling on the vase that she'd swapped out.

"W-where did you come from?" she said.

Karl stopped below the dais with the wedding table and looked up at her. "I could ask you the same question." Because whoever she was, she clearly didn't belong here. She had come in from the dry heat outdoors, unsuspecting of what the wedding venue held in store. Snow. Lots of it. If she were a wedding crasher, she was twenty-four hours too early to the party. And he frowned when he thought of the alternative. A thief under his nose.

A very alluring thief...

But a thief, nevertheless, he thought firmly, scowling.

"This is private property," he said. "I'm not sure how you passed building security, but your adventure ends here."

"My *adventure*?" she sputtered, somehow managing to sound indignant. As though she had the right to be offended.

Despite his best effort to be unaffected, a smile twitched at his lips. It was hard to clamp down on the sudden humor she provoked in him. But it would be harder for him to remain stern if he laughed now.

"Trespassing has to be a crime in Kenya too."

"I'm not trespassing!" She gripped the vase tighter. "I have a reason to be here."

He hadn't noticed her African accent, but it was more pronounced now. Possibly because a thread of wariness had crept into her voice. Studying her carefully, he realized he liked the way she looked. Even more than he had when he'd been observing from above, unnoticed. She had a lovely face. Soft in some areas, sharper and more defined in others. It wasn't long before he cataloged her wide-set eyes, a darker shade of brown that deceptively looked soul-piercingly black. Then there was her wide-tipped nose, low cheekbones, round lips and short, smooth chin, each part of her forever slotted in his memory. Normally he wouldn't be a stickler for those kinds of details. People didn't interest him the way event management did. Unlike coordinating events of any scale, people were...unpredictable. Untrustworthy.

Disruptive.

If he had a greater understanding of people, he'd have a better relationship with those he should've cared most about and who should care about him: his family.

But that was neither here nor there. Snapping

his attention up to her eyes again, Karl stoically confronted her glare.

"What could that reason be?" he asked, unfazed by her withering look.

She opened her mouth but snapped it shut when voices sounded from farther behind them.

Karl guessed the noise was coming from the building's entrance. Her widening eyes and startled expression told him that it could be security hunting for their intruder. With nowhere to run and hide, they'd find her soon enough. Unless he stepped aside and aided her escape. Something which he wouldn't do. No matter how panicked she appeared to be.

He scoffed. "I thought you had a reason to be here."

"I do," she said breathily. "I-I can explain. Really. But not now. Not *here*."

The voices were closing in, getting louder and more distinct. He could almost make out what they were saying.

"Please, let me go," she begged, a frantic air to her words.

Her plea wrenched sharply at his heart, surprising a grunt from him. It wasn't the words, exactly. Rather the emotion behind them. The way her brows pinched together, and her eyes grew round and unblinking with panic. It was a look he recognized subconsciously from his past. Without needing to ask her for clarification, he knew that she felt cornered and helpless.

Not helpless, he amended. She'd asked for his help. And he hadn't decided whether he was up to aiding and abetting her escape when he had been the one that had caught her.

Karl clenched his teeth, mulling over her request and his sudden indecision. He'd been certain that he wouldn't cave.

Yet that was what he was going to do.

"Hide." He spat the one word out before he regretted it.

Heeding his command, she scurried around the bridal party table, still carrying the vase, and ducked between the white opera chairs, out of sight.

Just in time too. They weren't alone anymore.

Turning to their new arrivals, Karl headed them off. The farther they were away from the head table, the better. He didn't even know her name or what her motive was, and here he was, covering for her.

I can explain, she'd said.

Her words felt honest. He chose to rely on them, and he never backtracked on a decision. He hadn't for a long time. Pushing away the memories of his unhappy childhood, he focused on the present.

On the people who had chased his mystery woman into hiding.

When did she become your *woman?*

Banishing that thought someplace dark and unvisited, he greeted the newcomers.

Istarlin cowered on the other side of the table, one hand securing the vase while the other clawed into the long silken gold tablecloth. She strained to hear the conversation happening only a few feet away. To think she'd been saved and spared by the gorgeous stranger even after he'd rudely accused her of being an intruder!

She wasn't breaking any law. Not when the vase belonged to her. Her intent hadn't been to steal anything at all. The vase wasn't perfect, and it had bugged her to know that it could be. Replacing it had been her sole goal. A quick in-and-out mission, but she hadn't anticipated being caught and questioned—and now cornered.

Though, to be fair, the stranger didn't know better. And she would have set him straight, but then she had heard her grandfather, and nothing else mattered except the urge to retreat.

Now her grandfather's booming voice spoke. "You're the wedding planner?"

"No, I'm not, but the event coordinator sent me in her place."

That voice she knew instantly too. How could she not, when he'd practically interrogated and scolded her like a child caught with her hand in a cookie jar? It was her handsome stranger.

Her stomach swooped at the thought of him, her face warming pleasantly and a dopey smile pulling her lips wide. After his rude insinuation and the haughty manner in which he had summarily chalked her up as a thief, she hadn't expected him to play chivalrous knight. Not that she'd been swooning. Nor had she been in any real danger. She had just not wanted to confront her grandfather, and she had the oddest sensation that the handsome stranger had known and commiserated with her reasoning.

Lin crouched lower with her vase, her attention vaulting back to the discussion on the other side of the table.

"You must be the bride." Her gorgeous stranger's smooth, dulcet voice had the same effect on her as a big mug of hot cocoa would after a cold day. She shivered from the rush of pleasure.

"Yes, I had hoped for a tour today. One last time before the big day tomorrow."

Lin smiled at the sound of her childhood friend, Machelle. The blushing bride-to-be.

Machelle's parents and Lin's grandfather were longtime friends and neighbors. Though Machelle's family were well-off, Lin's grandfather had generously offered to help pay for the wedding. She suspected that he knew what Machelle's friendship meant to her, and it was his way of showing he cared.

Still, when Machelle and her family had invited her to be part of today's tour of the venue and Lin had learned her grandfather would be going as well, the decision to decline the bride's invitation had been both easy and difficult. Easy because she hadn't wanted her grandfather to ply her with an endless stream of questions about her career plans, and Machelle had understood that. But difficult because she knew what this moment meant to her friend. They had been there for each other for almost their whole lives. Through all the highs and lows and heartbreaks and triumphs. They had attended university together too. Growing even closer over the past few years when they'd left their families behind to study abroad in Switzerland. It was there, while on a study break in the Swiss Alps at picturesque Zermatt, that Lin had watched Machelle fall in love with her husband-to-be.

And now they'd recreated that first meeting in a snow-capped mountain resort with this Swiss chalet–inspired venue. It was beautiful...but also very cold.

Another shiver raced through her, her teeth chattering lightly and her poor toes curling against the glacial air circulating in the building. She should have known to dress better. But stopping by her apartment for a change of clothes had felt like a waste of time. In hindsight, she'd have liked something big and warm like the Burberry woolen coat her good-looking stranger was wearing. She'd have recognized the designer label's check pattern on his upturned collar anywhere. Meaning he wasn't a broke stranger.

A wealthy wedding planner. Business had to be booming at his workplace.

Envy cut coldly through her warm, fluttery attraction to him. She couldn't help it. She'd been working her tail off to build the beginnings of her own business. The thought of someone else attaining a similar dream left her mouth tasting sour and her heart bitter.

She knew it was irrational to be jealous. She didn't want to be an event planner.

Her aspiration was in her arms and cradled close to her chest.

So why does it feel like it's slipping out of my grasp?

She had hit a metaphoric wall and stalled in her business plan.

And all because she didn't have the courage to face her grandfather.

Not entirely true.

She had faced him somewhat, but it was obvious to her that he wasn't serious about listening to her entrepreneurial planning. *He* was the wall she'd run headlong into and was finding hard to surmount.

The problem was that he had always been the no-nonsense type. He didn't see her renting a studio to produce her work as anything meriting recognition. In his eyes, she was dabbling at a hobby. He hadn't said it aloud, but she heard it nevertheless in the way he shut her out quietly whenever she broached the subject of becoming a business owner.

Now, if Lin worked at a reputable, successful place like where her handsome stranger worked, maybe she'd have avoided all this.

Wait!

She held still as her brain fired off a sudden plan.

What if she *did* work with him?

Lin perked up. Suddenly she bounded with energy. She could almost forget that her legs were beginning to cramp. Almost. She wasn't superhuman. Her calves burned, and her knees wobbled. If they didn't get going soon, she might just have to face the music and come out from hiding…

"I would be happy to host the tour. Let's begin with the ice sculptures in the freezer. They'll be displayed right before the reception begins," the stranger said, coming to her rescue for a second time.

She heard them leaving. Knew when it was the right time to peek over the table and stand and stretch her legs. Blissfully alone, Lin marched toward the exit, and before anyone could stop her, she escaped out of the snowy venue into the early-evening heat of Nairobi.

For a moment she soaked in the warmth, sighing happily as the cold entombing her limbs thawed. It was so nice to be outdoors again. She'd been freezing her buns off in there. Free of the chill holding her hostage, she raced away from the imposing building which occupied the larger part of the parking lot that it had been constructed on. She didn't stop until she crossed the street and slipped into the idling taxi that she had instructed to wait for her.

The cabbie beamed when she handed him the extra dollar bills for his trouble.

"Where to next, ma'am?"

Lin thought of several places she could go next. Looking down at her vase and then gazing at the sloping roof of the stone and wood building across the street, she settled on the place she wanted to be most right then.

"We'll stay here for a little longer. There's someone I'm waiting for."

She didn't elaborate, holding the image of the stranger's face in her mind. His very good-looking face. She had to be crazy. Drooling over the guy when he had been ready to assume the worst about her character. As far as first impressions went, it sucked.

Memorable, she conceded bitterly. Yet still awful. But she couldn't turn her back on the idea of working with his event-management company. Surely his boss would be willing to consider her business proposal…

She also was stumped as to why he had changed his mind and helped hide her.

The man was a conundrum. A coldly curt and very gorgeous enigma.

The meter ran for another hour before she sat up and gave the cab driver her next instruction.

"Follow that car." She pointed out the vehicle the stranger had gotten into when he'd walked out of the venue, unaccompanied by Lin's grandfather, Machelle or anyone else.

With a dip of his chin, the cabbie proceeded to shadow the shining black Lamborghini that roared out onto the street ahead of them. Wishing she'd sat up front with the driver, Lin flung off her seat belt and sat forward to keep her eyes on the car they were trailing closely. She wouldn't lose sight of him. Whoever he was. After all, she still owed him an explanation. More so now that he'd spared her an embarrassing moment with her grandfather.

She had plenty to say. And she'd start by thanking him.

CHAPTER TWO

RETURNING TO HIS hotel suite, he was left with a strong taste of defeat in his mouth.

Perplexed by the restlessness still pressing down on his shoulders, Karl tapped the passcode into the lighted keypad and opened the door to his rooms. His first stop was obvious: the bathroom. A splash of cold water over his face did nothing to clear his mind. Stripping off his coat, he tossed it over the bed and did something he normally never did: he left a trail of clothing to the shower. Sloppiness wasn't his MO. The only thing that kept him from falling apart was his persistent need to keep his life organized. Everything he did had purpose. Every task he set his mind to accomplish was a stepping-stone to greater things for him and his company. Every person in his life had a place and reason to matter to him. And he knew when it was the right time to cut off a relationship that wasn't going anywhere, be it romantic, platonic or business.

The problem was he couldn't fully control other people. Didn't know what they were thinking or planning. In his line of work, he could create a masterpiece of an event and still have a client suddenly decide that nothing he had done for them lived up to their expectations. It didn't happen often, but when it did, it almost always ruined his mood.

He couldn't manage some aspects of his personal life either. His family came to mind, his parents more specifically.

Karl curled his lip into a sneer at the thought of his mom and dad. Serenity and Charles Sinclair. He didn't think he'd ever meet anyone like them. And that wasn't a compliment. His parents had hearts colder and as unforgiving as a winter in the Arctic Circle. They hadn't ever tried to understand him, instead asserting their authority over him. They had attempted and failed to govern his life. When they had realized he wouldn't do as they said, they'd thrown him out of the family home. It had been the end of a string of unpleasant incidents that marked his childhood as unhappy and made him into the grudging adult he was today. He hated that they still provoked strong emotion in him. That was what he wished he could control most whenever he considered them.

With a grumble, he set the controls of the shower

panel to his preferred temperature and flow rate and turned the water on.

He couldn't control people...but he *could* dampen the effect they had on him. One tactic he used was to push inconsequential encounters out of his mind. Strangers shouldn't warrant his time and effort.

Strangers like the pretty woman from the wedding venue.

He snapped his teeth together hard. Why had he suddenly thought of her?

Even as he berated himself silently, he thought of her again when he stepped under the shower-head. Water pelted over his knotted muscles, ridding him of most of his tension but not washing away the underlying unease that had grafted onto him at the venue. It started right about the time he had left the bride and her tour party behind and found the wedding hall empty. The only trace his mystery woman had been there was the swapped vase.

She is a thief, then. Report her and be done with it.

Easier said than done. It was too simple a solution, and one that didn't appease his jitteriness.

He exited the shower, a towel covering him, and felt as anxious as he did when he'd walked into his room. Spotting the crystal decanter on the sideboard in the sitting room, he turned in that direction. Perhaps a drink would blow the fog from his mind. Karl poured himself two fingers of brandy and leaned into the burn sliding smoothly down his throat. Another glass almost had him believing he was all right.

Dropping his towel from his waist, he dressed methodically, his mind absent and his heart troubled by the questions he'd likely never have answered now. He forced himself to concentrate on what mattered most: seeing that everything went uninterrupted tomorrow. Today's mistake wouldn't be repeated. He had seen to that by briefing security to buff up their surveillance with round-the-clock monitoring, more muscle and a no-tolerance policy on any other party-crashers.

Even a certain pretty one if she were to show her face again.

Taking a breath, he battled the instinct to think of her anymore. What he needed was a distraction. A suitable one that would get his mind onto business that was far more productive.

A glance at his laptop gave him an idea of what he could occupy himself with. His godmother, Carrie, had hired him to plan an event for her that would take place in a few months, at the end of December. As she was important to him, he'd poured himself into the project personally. But it had become that much more crucial when Karl had learned Carrie had invited his parents to the event. Since they'd tossed him out of the house, his mother and father hadn't made any effort to speak with him, least of all inquire about his business. What they had wanted was for him and his four siblings to join Sinclair Corp., the family conglomerate in the real estate and construction industries. Only his older brother, Cyrus, had eventually done as their parents had envisioned for their children. His younger sister, Cherelle, lived as a Canadian expat with her husband and children in Qatar. Meanwhile, his younger twin brothers, Solomon and Simon, had moved out for college and managed a thriving social-media presence as lifestyle influencers.

His parents had been less than thrilled. In their eyes, most of their children had grown to be failures. All but Cyrus, who had followed along with their plans like the good little sheep that he was.

They'd cut Karl off from his trust fund—like he had cared. And it had been the same for his siblings.

Although these days he barely kept in touch with his sister and brothers, Karl had known that their mom and dad hadn't been kind to them either, financially. Not that they'd ever displayed any kindness in their lives apart from their annual corporate charity gala and the occasional philanthropic business venture. But he knew that was more for press politics than out of the milk of human kindness.

It was that lack of compassion he blamed for the lack of closeness to his siblings.

On top of training them to be little drones, their parents had gone out of their way to ensure their children knew who their closest competition was in life: each other. All their lives they'd been pitted against one another, from excelling in school grades to being the top in their approved extracurricular activities. More times it was Cyrus, their golden Sinclair heir, that had been raised to be the eyes, ears and mouthpiece of their mom and dad. Tattling, taunting, spying—none of it was out-of-bounds to Cyrus so long as he did as their parents said and reported back any insurgence that Karl and his other siblings might have in mind.

Cyrus had also turned his back on him when their parents had ousted him from the house.

Karl had never forgiven him for it.

I probably won't ever, he thought darkly of his older brother.

He didn't know if Cyrus would be present at their godmother's party, but if he were, he'd be treated as coolly as their parents. There was no love lost between them. Just anger and questions, starting with how Cyrus could be so disloyal to the younger siblings he should have instead protected.

Karl dismissed his useless thinking, knowing he'd get no peace or answers, and considered what his godmother's event could be for him. He was planning it primarily as a labor of love. Carrie had been the parental figure he'd wished he had instead of his own cold, loveless parents. She had encouraged him to move in with her when he'd been tossed out on his ear. He had been a confused, heartbroken twenty-year-old with no home suddenly. She'd paid for his plane ticket from his home in Toronto to Calgary. There, she had opened the door to her warm home and seen that he finished his last two years of college. It was also Carrie who had opened his eyes to his passion in event planning and coordinating. One Christmas, she'd asked him to help her plan a large holiday gathering, and he had found it a real joy to put together the event and oversee its ultimate success. And it was Carrie who had pushed him to open the doors on Heartbeat Events when he'd first confided in her about his initial idea. Without her, he might have turned out to be exactly who his parents had hoped he would become without their support: a nobody and a failure.

He owed Carrie more than one party. He owed

her the devotion he'd wished he had gotten from his mom and dad and Cyrus.

Naturally, besides being a gift for his godmother, it was also the perfect chance to finally exact his brand of vengeance on his parents. He would show his mom and dad that he had thrived without their confidence and support. Once they saw he was living well, he'd have the best kind of revenge.

With that thinking in mind, falling into work was easy. He didn't move from the desk even when he placed a call for room service. Finally, a knock on the door turned his attention away from reading his high-priority emails.

Room service was quicker than he'd anticipated.

Relieved that he wouldn't be disturbed again for the evening, Karl answered the door before the second knock came, fully expecting to have his dinner dropped off and to be left alone.

"You," was the first word that forced its way out of his mouth.

The pretty thief from the wedding venue stood outside his suite, and she looked perfectly comfortable disrupting his privacy. His hand gripped the door tighter, his lower jaw rock-hard, and his heart—to his great annoyance—racing faster with what he swore was exhilaration. Pure, unfiltered, lust-ridden *excitement*.

What was wrong with him? He should have been calling Reception and asking for security to be brought up to escort her away. Instead, he was standing there like a statue, watching as she sized him up from head to toe. A strange, hot anticipation pinched at his skin, and his mouth grew dry as he fought for words.

"Who are you?" he all but growled, demanding an answer.

A smile danced over her glossed lips, her loveliness becoming more…lovely.

He nearly rolled his eyes at his cheesy thinking.

Clearly my brain's turning to mush.

Still smiling, she said, "Oh, that's right. We never introduced ourselves. I'm Istarlin Mohamed. Nobody calls me by my full name, though. It's just Lin, normally."

There was nothing normal about this.

He forced composure into his voice—and pushed away thoughts of how delectable her mouth looked when she pursed her lips just so. Biting the words out, he asked, "How did you find me?"

Her smile grew wider. "That part was surprisingly easy."

"Oh, really?" He clenched his teeth, confused as to whether he should be amused or annoyed. First the security at the venue had failed, and now his hotel was seriously flunking in privacy measures too. He was beginning to suspect she had a knack for showing up in places she shouldn't be. Like his hotel room.

"Let me rephrase my question. Why are you here?"

She looked him over, and he wondered what she saw; her poker face would kill him. "I promised you an explanation, didn't I?"

She had, but he hadn't really expected one. That was his error in judgment.

Feeling her eyes rake over him once again, he stood taller and recalled that not too long ago he'd been strutting around his suite in nothing but a Turkish-cotton towel. Oddly the thought of her catching him in the buff didn't displease him. Even more strangely, he felt disappointed that their second meeting hadn't unfolded in that way.

"Aren't you going to invite me in?"

He pointedly stared at the decorative vessel she was hugging to her chest. "I'd rather just take the vase you stole."

"I told you I'm not a thief. Nothing was stolen."

Karl raised an eyebrow.

She rolled her eyes, something he wasn't used to others doing around him. When he talked, people often listened intently. Maybe he'd been surrounding himself with sycophants. Or maybe this woman marched to her own drum. Again, instead of it upsetting him, the notion intrigued him. Made her that much more interesting.

"What I have to say can be said in the hall too, you know. I have nothing to be embarrassed about." She looked over her shoulder, smiling brightly suddenly. "Did you order room service?"

A hotel staff member pushed a fully stocked meal-service cart toward his suite.

"Is that pilau?" She licked her lips, the slow drag of her pink tongue more enticing than the tantalizing scents wafting from the service cart.

Tipping the hotel employee, Karl said, "That'll be all, thank you."

Once they were alone, he rolled the cart into his room and wasn't surprised when Lin trailed him inside. Uninvited. Realizing that he wouldn't be rid of her *or* his insistent fascination for her, he threw in the towel and gave her what she wanted. An audience.

"Fine. Let's hear this explanation."

Lin paced, not because it helped calm her strung-out nerves but rather because it gave her something to focus on. And this way she wasn't sitting across from him at the dining table and under his intense scrutiny. She didn't think anyone had a right to have such a powerfully commanding aura to them. Well, outside her grandfather.

"Like I said earlier, I was never an intruder. I couldn't be because I know the bride. She's a close friend of mine."

"Why hide from her, then?" He seared her with his implacable gaze.

The mercy he had shown her in the wedding venue was gone in that moment. It was obvious he wanted it all. Every detail that would clear her name in his eyes. She shouldn't have cared what he thought. If she hadn't followed him, would they ever see each other again? Even at the wedding tomorrow, the odds they'd run into each other with Machelle's crazy-long guest list were slim. Yet here she was, invading his private space, with the sole intent of rectifying their first impression of each other.

Mostly his impression of her.

It wouldn't do for him to think she was a thief or an interloper. Not if they would be working together…but she hadn't gotten to that part yet. Also, if she were being honest with herself, she sensed he was a good person. Despite all his scowling, and the little bit of growling he'd done when he had opened the door to find her there, Lin just knew that under his gruff, coldly smart exterior beat a good heart. With that stout certainty backing her, she had even indulged in looking at him like a woman might her lover. She openly eyed all his yumminess but stopped at outright flirting with him. Because if he didn't flirt back, it'd sink her chances at repairing his opinion of her *and* she could kiss goodbye any chance of working with him.

She gulped quietly and remembered he had asked a question.

"I wasn't hiding from her. It was my grandfather that I was avoiding." Just as she avoided direct eye contact with her wondrously hot stranger and now host. Swallowing nervously, she explained, "It's complicated, but I have my reasons for doing what I did."

"Your grandfather is Salim Mohamed?"

She nodded, knowing what was coming.

"The cement and sugar tycoon of Kenya."

She bobbed her head again, wincing but adding, "Actually, it's the cement and sugar *lord* of Kenya. A subtle difference, *tycoon* and *lord*."

Talking about her grandfather was difficult these days. Though her favorite person in the world, he had been a large part of her distressing soul-searching journey of late.

"So the bride is your friend." Gesturing to the vase she'd placed on the table, he said, "I'm sure the vase has a story too."

"I made it. It's one of my 3D-printed designs." Machelle had been the biggest supporter of her

3D art when Lin had stumbled into the world of printed materials a year ago. Lin had been hooked instantly. So much so that she had sunk a pretty penny into buying studio space for her printers far from her grandfather's luxurious mansion. It was also the studio that had saved her from spending awkward nights at home after arguments with him.

Not that they *had* to argue. All she wanted from him was to hear her out. Why was it so hard for him to understand she wasn't as passionate about cement and sugar as he was? That had to be a qualification for becoming the new chairperson and president of his multimillion-dollar company.

"You created it?" The first note of interest edged his tone as he grasped the vase and considered it with furrowed eyebrows. Tracing his fingers over the thin gold metal strands forming the ornamental container, he asked, "This was made with a printer?"

"A very expensive printer with very pricey material, yes."

"And the bride requested you to make them for her wedding?"

"She's my friend, and I wanted to do something for her."

"Why take your gift away, then?"

"It hadn't printed perfectly." She pointed to the

base where the printer had missed a small space in the net of thin, sticklike strands. Hardly noticeable to the untrained eye, but it bugged her to know the mistake existed. Made her feel like the possibility of selling her 3D designs was a stupid fantasy. "I wanted to replace it before anyone noticed the mistake."

"But I caught you," he finished and placed the creation back down. "It also doesn't explain why you're here."

She stopped pacing and exhaled slowly. "You work for the wedding-planning company, right?"

"We do all events, not just weddings."

Lin smiled meekly, the shyness creeping on her faster. This part would be the hardest to say.

I have to try, though.

"You wouldn't happen to be looking for designers to collaborate with, would you? A contractual basis would be fine. It's not like I need worker benefits or anything." Gee. Did she sound shrill and desperate? Yes, and yes.

Tossing shame aside, she continued her rambling. "I can assure you my 3D art works well for other event decor. Table numbering, photo-booth props, cake toppers, name tags and hanging decorations. Even jewelry. I've done a few pieces. Earrings, a necklace and an anklet."

"An anklet," he murmured after her, sliding his hands off the table and standing.

Worrying that she was losing his interest, Lin babbled on. "If that's your thing, yes. But I could see bigger, more important pieces like tiaras for the brides and bow ties and cuff links for the grooms." She looked at him, awed again by the body-slamming desire she experienced the first time she'd seen him—and each time after that. Bald men normally didn't do it for her, outside of the droolworthy god that was Shemar Moore.

But there was a sexy edge to the sharpness of his dark slanted eyebrows and piercing black-brown eyes, the set of his Roman nose, the rosiness of his Cupid's-bow mouth and well-defined, angular cheekbones and clean-shaven jawline. What did it for her best, though, was the thick but well-trimmed black mustache that made her envision kissing him and feeling the rough tickling brush of his facial hair along her upper lip—

Her mouth tingled as if touched.

"I-I hoped you could give me your boss's contact information."

"For a job," he clarified.

Nodding, she held her breath and waited.

He didn't leave her in suspense for long. Following a slight pause, he moved for the serving cart holding his dinner. "I'll admit, I'm intrigued. I would have to hear more, though."

Had she heard him correctly? "Wait. You're the boss?"

"I am."

That…wasn't what she expected at all. But it suited his authoritative attitude. And it explained why he'd been so presumptive and bossy with her, and why he had cared that she might be a gate-crasher at the venue.

"Is that a problem?" He faced her now, his plate in hand and a brow raised in challenge.

"No." But her stomach churned from the news. From delight or mortification, she didn't know.

"As I said, I'd want to know more of what this partnership would look like. Seeing as your friend's wedding is tomorrow, I'll be busy. My only free slot would be the day after tomorrow. It'd have to be the morning, as I have a flight home later in the day."

Lin bobbed her head, processing his flurry of instructions slowly and quietly.

"Is that all?" he asked, his tone matching his neutral expression.

Understanding she'd outstayed her welcome, and not wanting to irritate him to the point of canceling their business meeting, she hurried for the exit. But she whirled back to him in the hall, feeling him close behind her. "I didn't catch your name."

"It's Karl," he told her before handing her the vase she'd almost left behind in her haste.

"Karl." She tested his name on her tongue and liked the feel of it. "It's a pleasure to meet you, and hopefully it'll be a pleasure to work with you too." She sounded as nervous as she felt. And the nerves continued to assail her as she left the hotel and caught a taxi. She wondered if it would be like this all the time, and if so, whether she'd taken on a greater challenge where Karl was concerned.

CHAPTER THREE

IT WAS AN unusual and frustrating sensation for him to be nervous, but Karl couldn't deny that he was a little on edge about this meeting with Istarlin Mohamed.

Lin, he corrected in his mind, recalling that she'd seemed to prefer the nickname. He found it irritating too that he liked the sound of it. That he found her name as beautiful as she was.

He had to stop thinking that way, though. If this meeting panned out well, she could be working with him. What she didn't need was her boss secretly lusting after her. He wouldn't make her uncomfortable.

Or complicate my own life, for that matter, he thought with stony finality.

All he had to do was remind himself that she wasn't any different from the countless people he met in his line of work. Through Heartbeat Events, he'd had the pleasure of planning and coordinating events of elite caliber for individuals from loftier walks of life: popular celebrities and star athletes, dignitaries from the world over and inspirational activists. Lin was no different than the well-heeled heiresses he'd met before. They had been stunning in looks and dress too.

But he hadn't wanted to haul any of those other heiresses up against his chest and kiss them on their prettily glossed lips, now, had he?

Karl blew out a slow, strained breath full of his frustration. Fine. He was attracted to her more fiercely than he had felt about anyone in a long while. He could remember only one other time that he'd experienced a similar force of physical desire for another.

Isaiah.

The name passed through his mind more easily than it had before. Soon as he thought of his past lover, he pushed the comparison aside. Lin wasn't Isaiah. And this wasn't the same attraction—at least he wouldn't allow it to flourish in the way that it had with his college ex-boyfriend.

Cooling his nerves and his heated lustful thinking for the woman he was meeting, Karl concentrated on his surroundings.

Nairobi had the same hyped-up energy as his home in Calgary. The East African city was alive in its own right. The buildings breathing and the paved roads thumping with life force.

The sky was mostly blue again, and the weather temperate for September. It helped calm him knowing that he didn't have to worry about the weather on his short trip there. Even if he did, he wouldn't be able to control the climate like the other factors in his life. Although, he wasn't doing any better there.

Like the climate, I can't seem to control what I feel for Lin.

Ignoring the confused desperation in that thought, he realized he was closing in on the meeting place.

"Right there," he instructed the driver, the GPS on his phone pinging with the alert that he was close to his destination. When the cabbie told him that he couldn't get any closer, Karl paid his fare and exited the car, figuring a short walk wouldn't hurt. But almost as soon as he opened the car door, he had to slam it shut when an auto rickshaw roared past dangerously close. The cab driver had a chuckle at his expense, leaving Karl even more irate than how he'd woken up. Crossing the street more carefully, he made it to the overly populated sidewalk and steeled himself for the squeeze through pedestrians thronging all corners of the bustling neighborhood.

Reading again the text Lin had sent him, he followed her guideposts to a two-story building with faded signage and an empty commercial space for lease on the first level. The front entrance was locked. He tried the buzzer, his impatience heightening the uncomfortable and odd anxiety he'd been battling all the way here.

"Yes?" Lin's voice rang like birdsong through the small, stuffy enclosure. He hadn't noticed how pleasing her voice was.

Gritting his teeth and clenching his fists, he barked, "It's Karl. I'm here for our meeting."

She didn't reply, but a second later a tonal buzz indicated that she'd unlocked the entrance for him.

The stairs were the only option. It was a short flight to the second level, his path barred by a door. He rapped his knuckles on the door sharply and rattled the metal frame.

Lin's flushed face was the first thing he saw when she threw open the door, her brown cheeks rosier, and her eyes bright and lively, her smile shining as hot as the early September morning. "Oops, I lost track of the time. I hope you haven't had trouble with directions."

She gestured for him to come through, talking a mile a minute and with a chirpiness that no amount of coffee could give him, not even on his best of days.

He hadn't seen her since yesterday when he'd glimpsed her briefly at her friend's wedding.

They both had been busy: Lin celebrating with her friend, while he ensured that the reception started and ended on the same high note. He'd indicated they wouldn't have a chance to speak all night, and it had been true. But now, with the wedding and their commitments out of the way, they had nothing but the rest of the morning with each other. No interruptions in sight. And later he'd catch his long first-class flight back home.

"Let me just grab my purse, and we can head out." She cast him another sunny smile and then flitted off to do as she said, leaving him in the large, open space to explore and get a feel for who she was. Boxy industrial windows allowed a generous amount of sunlight into the unit and lit up the darker cement walls. The lightly varnished hardwood flooring shone like new. Large machines were neatly arranged behind a workbench. He walked over to what he assumed were the 3D printers. They had all sorts of nuts and bolts and looked more complicated than he'd thought printers ought to be. He recalled how impassioned she'd looked discussing her 3D art two days ago in his hotel room. Now he envisioned her toiling away in the space and with nothing but her craft to keep her company. The feeling felt familiar. It had been that familiarity that had him curious enough to venture out to meet her rather than canceling on her at the very last minute.

Before he delved into the reasoning behind that thought, he spun away from her printers at the sound of clicking heels on the wood floors.

Lin emerged out of the only other room in the space, her face still flushed and a purse in her hands. Hooking a thumb over her shoulder, she asked, "Did you want to see some of the pieces I have stored away?"

He followed her into what she was using as a storage space…and a bedroom, apparently. A pillow and a blanket lay on a leather recliner squeezed into a corner of the room. It almost appeared as if she'd just woken up. She hadn't even had the time to fold her blanket.

Reading his thoughts, she said, "I work late sometimes. Too late for me to travel home and worry about waking my grandfather. So I just stay here."

Karl supposed it explained the makeshift sleeping quarters. He'd had his bouts of working late into the night, so he spared his judgment on her.

Casting his gaze from the sofa to the metal shelves lining the other side of the room, he was awed by all the items she'd produced. The shelves were laden with all sorts of different pieces in varying sizes, colors and even textures.

"Silver?" He picked up a palm-sized owl

figurine that had caught his eye. The detailing work on the figure was precise and exquisite.

"Yes. It's a paperweight. It was my first attempt at printing and casting a mold for sterling silver." She glanced away shyly and said, "I don't think it turned out that great."

Karl stared at her, sensing that she wasn't fishing for compliments but that she truly believed that she'd fallen short of excellence when nothing could be further from the truth. Without thinking, he ventured an opinion.

"I've never been big on beginner's luck. That's just a lazy way of saying you're good at what you're doing. And, clearly, you have a strong talent for what you do."

Their eyes met, and a spasm of electrified lust shot through him. He stiffened from head to toe and clutched onto her well-made silver paperweight like it was a lifeline. It was hard to tell what she was thinking or feeling: her face gave nothing away.

Then she blinked, smiled and moved for the door. "We can talk more outside. I don't want to keep you any longer than I have already."

The momentary respite he'd found in Lin's studio vanished when he set foot outside with her by his side.

"Is it always like this, or have we hit the tourist patch of the city?" Karl hadn't made it a point to research Nairobi beyond its temperature and climate. He had wanted to dress practically. Tourism hadn't been a consideration.

Lin grinned at him. "Eastleigh is always like this. Open day and night, business at all hours, and business brings people."

He grunted, figuring he'd have to get used to the jostling bodies all around them as he kept up with her pace. She walked with purpose. And he had no doubt that he could rest easy and let her lead him to their next destination. It was strange for him to allow someone else to take control. He always preferred remaining in charge, knowing what could happen when power and control had been used against him. His parents had abused his trust enough times to brand the lesson into him. Whenever Karl wanted to do anything for himself, they were always there to remind him that not only should he listen to them but that without them he would amount to nothing. That he'd *be* nothing.

Tucking aside the unpleasant thoughts about his mom and dad before they fully resurfaced, he concentrated on his surroundings and on the gorgeous woman who was walking alongside him. What he didn't want to think about was the contradictions in his behavior. Didn't want to contemplate what Lin had to do with the uncharacteristic changes he'd been dealing with when he was around her.

It didn't stop him from sneaking glances at her.

She sensed his stare and locked eyes with him. "Did you want a quick walking tour before we head to the restaurant? I know you're leaving Nairobi by the end of the day, but it'd be a shame to miss the city."

They'd decided their meeting could happen over breakfast. The idea of using his time efficiently always appealed to him. He appreciated that Lin felt the same way.

"A walking tour sounds good."

She beamed at that, falling into her role of impromptu tour guide with a graceful ease. He followed her closely as she pointed to the places they passed. To his immediate right, the gated sandy-stoned building with large open doors and a blue domed spire was a well-visited mosque in the area. The row of shops to her left were largely owned by Somali immigrants and locals who formed an overwhelmingly large part of the population in Eastleigh.

"And up ahead we'll catch the *matatu* out of Eastleigh and to the restaurant."

Dust swirled up from the corners of the sidewalk and flooded his lungs with a grainy sensation. He coughed, and she pulled a plastic baggie full of masks from her purse. She handed him one. "Newcomers might be irritated by the dust. It's harder on your lungs than it is on ours."

"It's everywhere," he remarked from behind the safety of his mask, his eyes still stinging from the sandy grains in the air.

"Eastleigh wasn't like this always. My grandfather tells me it was much greener when he was a young boy." Her accent was soft but pronounced, and her voice lyrical and sweet to his ears. He could close his eyes and listen to her talk all day—

Karl pulled the brake on his thinking. They had come together for business. He wasn't in the market for romantic entanglements. Certainly not with a woman he'd not only just met but whose services he was considering hiring for his company. She couldn't be more off-limits right then.

If a forbidden workplace romance didn't put him off, all he had to do was recall that he'd compared his instant and powerful attraction to her to what he'd had with his only serious lover, Isaiah.

And it hadn't ended well with Isaiah.

No, it hadn't, and though his heartbreak had passed when his ex-boyfriend had dumped him, the scar of it rested atop the emotional wounds his parents had left him with as well. All solid reminders that he couldn't control anyone—not the people he loved and not love itself from inflicting its damage on him.

He wouldn't add Lin to that mess, out of regard for her and as protection for himself.

Unaware of his inner turmoil, she continued with her tour. "Eventually Eastleigh became a business center, and with that the original residents of this enclave were pushed out, as were the trees and any greenery. All of that replaced by buildings, buildings and more buildings." She gestured to the infrastructure crammed into every available space in the area. If there had been green pastures here once, there was no indication of them now. "But the people are friendly and hardworking, and I couldn't have found a better place or price for my studio."

Just as she said that, a young man called to her from one of the shops they were passing.

"Lin, how have you been?"

Lin stopped to chat with him in another language. Karl gave them space and seized the chance to study her undisturbed. She had changed her hair yesterday for the wedding. Her sleek bob had become a wealth of silken raven-black coils she'd tempered with a large butterfly clip at the back of her head. She had on a simple white T-shirt with designer straight crop jeans and slip-on leather sandals that had him admiring her nude-colored toenails. When she laid her hand on the man's arm, a sourness flavored Karl's mouth. He recognized it as jealousy—which was wildly off base. He didn't know her. Had no claim to her. And if she were flirting with the other man, it had nothing to do with him.

But that rationality didn't erase the jealousy. It lingered like the dust riding the air. An irritant that perturbed him more deeply than he thought possible. He folded his arms, clenched his jaws and shifted his weight from foot to foot. The more he watched them, the more his bitterness became apparent.

Pleasantries exchanged, Lin gave the man a wave and fell back into line with Karl.

"As I was saying, the neighbors are a huge appeal to the area. Everyone's just trying to make a living here, and sometimes a little help along the way can make a difference."

"You seemed close," he observed, irked that he was still recalling her hand on the other man's arm.

"He helped find my studio."

"You weren't speaking Swahili." He'd been listening to the locals enough to recognize that she wasn't speaking the language.

"I'm ethnically Somali, but my family's lived in Kenya for decades, and it's the only home I've known."

They reached the end of the road, and Lin guided him to a white-hooded, colorfully painted bus. Political and social logos splashed the bus's exterior in harmonious graffiti art. He'd seen nothing like it before. "The *matatu*," she said, climbing the steps into it ahead of him. She paid the driver and grabbed a seat. He followed, realizing that she'd footed his fare as well. Squeezing into the bus seat with her had them shoulder to shoulder and closer than ever. The option of snagging the empty bench seat across from them had struck him, but his feet had carried him to her, and now that he was seated it would have been too awkward to move away.

At first, he looked everywhere but at her. The interior of the vehicle was painted as artfully inside as it was outside. TV screens were mounted above the seats, and the lights and sound system were in sync with the music that thumped out of the speakers. When he'd had his fill of gawking at the newness of his environment, he had nothing else to do but to strike up a conversation.

"Why 3D printing?"

A thoughtful look crossed her face before she answered, "I fell into it, and it makes me happy."

"You're good at it, too." That was no empty compliment either. From what he had seen of her finished products in her studio, she had talent and the skills to match. And there was no doubt in his mind she had the enthusiasm if she were willing to sleep rough in her studio. It led him to the question he'd been turning over in his mind since she had come to him in his hotel the day before yesterday. "You seem to have everything you need to make this work right here. Why are you looking for a job elsewhere?"

A pensive look crossed her face. "It's a long story better told over a meal."

CHAPTER FOUR

THE RESTAURANT WASN'T any different than it had been the last time Lin had visited—which wasn't too long ago. The menu had the same offerings, and the items she usually ordered were all priced similarly. Same four walls and wooden tables with plastic-covered chairs. The exact same view of Kenyatta Avenue, the central business district's main street, from where they sat under the canopy of the restaurant's patio.

Yes, everything's the same...except him. Karl.

Being close to him and having that intense personality of his homed in on her had her stomach in knots. She blushed furiously under his scrutinizing gaze. And though the dry autumn breeze hit her cheeks more coolly under the shade, it didn't quell the bubbling heat of her nerves entirely. And the anxiousness and physical awareness of their proximity became worse after she and Karl placed their orders with the waiter.

He sipped at his ice water, his eyes holding her gaze the whole time. "I've been trying a lot of Kenyan dishes."

She happily glommed on to the small talk, encouraging him with a smile and a nod. This she could do. Food was a safer topic. Less personal. "Have you found a favorite dish yet?"

"The pilau is something I'd like to recreate in my kitchen."

"It's a staple. I've tried it both with and without the meat and potatoes, with plenty of spices and very little seasoning, and it's always tasty. You can't go wrong with it."

"I would've ordered it if you hadn't influenced me to try something new." Then the corners of his mouth kicked up into the briefest but sexiest smile. There and gone by the time she blinked. She couldn't even be certain he had smiled.

She discreetly swiped her clammy palms down her legs. Taking a gulp of her glass of water, she worked around the lump in her throat to speak. "You'll like the meat stew, *mukimo*, and chapatis."

"I'll take your word for it." Again, she swore he flashed her a smile, but his face switched back to his default stoic expression too quickly.

When their order arrived, Lin had thought they were in the clear. She didn't relish the idea of speaking around a full mouth. But Karl seemed only to have gotten started.

"You never answered my question," he said, his fork scooping up the traditional green side dish of *mukimo* on his plate. He didn't blink when he popped the mixture of potato, peas and corn into his mouth. Just as fluidly, he tore off a piece of the chapati as she'd done and scooped up the meat stew on his plate with it. She sat and watched him eat, his stare never leaving her face.

Tearing her gaze away, she grasped her water glass and drank before replying. "What did you want to know again?"

"Just why you're looking to work someplace else. From what I've seen of your studio, you could start your own business."

"That's the goal." Though, she wished it were as simple as that.

In theory, she should have had no problem leaping into being a business owner. She had the passion, the plan she'd been working on for over the last six months, and money wasn't an issue either. She was an heiress to her grandfather's fortune. His only grandchild. And she'd known most her life that she would inherit his wealth, properties and other assets. She also knew she was the only choice her grandfather had ever had in mind to lead his company. That kind of pressure put a lot of weight on her shoulders.

A ton of weight on my heart, too, she thought sadly.

"But it's complicated," she added.

"You've said that before," he reminded her.

She recalled that she had, in his hotel suite. "I...have expectations on me. You met my grandfather."

The thought of her grandfather's powerful personality sharing a space with Karl's same level of energy and intensity made her a little dizzy. Luckily she didn't have to worry about that with Karl on his way home, and her grandfather busy planning out the rest of her life for her. At least careerwise. He hadn't shown too much interest in her romantic life. Not that he had to when there was an assumption she would marry well. And there wasn't a lack of men who fit that tall bill working for her grandfather.

"This isn't a public thing, so I hope you'll keep it between us," she began.

He soaked another piece of chapati, the unleavened flatbread passing his thick dusky-brown lips and mesmerizing her with the simple action. She gave her head a quick shake, patted her mouth with a napkin to be sure she hadn't dribbled anything and picked up her train of thought.

"My grandfather's planning his retirement."

He hadn't announced it yet. And it wouldn't happen overnight by any means. But she understood his retirement was in the near future. In two or three years, her life could change drastically. With him stepping down, she was expected to take over, and it scared her because it wasn't what she wanted.

"And you're his heir," said Karl, unsurprisingly connecting the dots and saving her the trouble of explaining that part.

She leaped into the rest of it with an ease that should have startled her. At least, it gave her pause to wonder who he was for her to feel so comfortable confiding in him. "My grandfather set his mind on it when he adopted me."

"Your parents?" he asked.

"My dad passed away, and my mom had filed for divorce and left us before he got sick." It popped out of her mouth, almost as easily as everything else had. She didn't talk about it often. Not because she hated to but because she didn't know what to make of it. She hadn't been in control of either her father dying when she'd been eight or her mother walking out on them when she'd been only two years old. If it hadn't been for her grandfather, she'd have been an orphan. Her dad had no siblings. She hadn't met any distant cousins, uncles or aunts. Only her grandfather. Though he hadn't ever showed how hard it had been on him to lose his son and suddenly be caring for his young granddaughter, Lin could only imagine the difficulties he'd had to bear quietly and stoically. He hadn't had the luxury of falling apart on her. She'd have been too young to understand and was grieving the loss of her dad.

As she grew older, she'd learned that her grandfather had lost his wife to childbirth a long time ago. So not only had he been handling the tragic passing of his wife but he had also shouldered the burden all parents feared in the premature death of his son.

Sometimes, when he thought she wasn't watching, she'd notice a distant, sorrowful look in his eyes. She noticed it happened more whenever she mentioned her dad. Without needing to ask explicitly, she knew he had to be mourning both her late grandmother and father.

Even with all her understanding and compassion, Lin couldn't know fully what he was feeling. She hadn't felt the love that he had once had and lost, especially his love for his wife.

She hadn't fallen in love yet. She'd dated, sure. But had she loved any of her dates? No. Some had been pleasant enough for her to want to see again, but she hadn't ever felt that spark, that bone-deep, soul-charging connection that fairy tales were all about, and it had steered her from many relationships that might have turned out to be...decent. Maybe not romances that were mindlessly passionate, but she could have had a companionable partnership with someone by now.

Deep down, if she were being more open with herself, she was a bit scared of falling in love. She'd seen how love had brought misery to her grandfather, and to herself when she'd lost her dad.

She hadn't wondered too much about her mom, but a small, secret part of her questioned whether her mother had stopped loving her all these years—or had it been that she had never loved her from the start? Lin knew she could go see her and ask. After Lin's dad passed away, her mom hadn't shown up for the funeral, but she would keep in touch with Lin's grandfather. For what? Lin hadn't ever asked or pursued the subject. She'd been just as fearful then to confirm that her mom might not want her. Being twenty-five now hadn't changed that. In some ways, she was still that sad, confused eight-year-old standing by her stern-faced grandfather as she said goodbye to her dad one last time.

She blinked sharply, the stark image of her dad's burial mound vanishing, and the restaurant and Karl calling her back from her reverie.

"Sorry for your loss," he said deeply and clearly.

Reflex kicked in, and she painted on a smile. "It was a long time ago."

"Still. Losing family is a challenge whose effects can ripple through the rest of our lives." Karl's response was unique. It fit his whole look and attitude, or what she'd experienced of him thus far. He looked at ease in his dove-gray polo shirt and slim-fit chinos, like she hadn't added her hectic past to their menu. Leaning back in his chair, he steepled his hands over his flat stomach and quietly assessed her.

He did that for a while before he remarked, "You have something to prove."

A blush stole over her cheeks again. It was hard not to be embarrassed when he had read her correctly. It was also a relief that she didn't have to explain herself. She'd been doing enough of that lately with her grandfather, trying to make him see her perspective. Having Karl understand her so readily was nice.

More than nice, she thought warmly.

Also, it got them to the heart of why she'd offered her 3D designing and printing services to his event-management company. "I love doing what I do in my studio. But if I were to open a business someday, I wouldn't be able to run my grandfather's company."

"Where does my company fit into your plan?"

"I want to see if I could do this professionally.

I've had a few orders from friends, and then there was Machelle's wedding, but I haven't done anything large-scale beyond that. Your company's well-established, and it caters to clients who have the pockets to host big parties. That means plenty of network opportunities and a chance to showcase my designs."

"You've given it a lot of thought," he drawled.

Cheeks still flushed and hot, Lin murmured, "Consider it my pitch."

He lapsed into a thoughtful silence and then said, "I do have an upcoming project that could work."

She sat up in her chair, pushed aside her plate and bobbed her head eagerly for him to continue.

"My godmother is renewing her marriage vows to her husband. The event is Kwanzaa-themed, so it's scheduled for the end of December."

"Kwanzaa?"

"I'm not surprised you haven't heard of it. It's a seven-day, pan-African celebration that's almost exclusively observed in North America. It's supposed to uplift the African culture and community over the weeklong festivities. It also happens to be my godmother's favorite holiday besides Christmas.

"I'd require a quick turnaround and a guarantee of quality from you. Also, the winter holiday season is our busiest, so we'll need to time-manage accordingly."

"Okay," she agreed, prepared to work around a tighter schedule. This was all a part of doing business. Working under all sorts of pressure and time constraints to deliver high-caliber and uniform goods.

"One more thing. You'd have to move offices."

She jerked back. "What?"

"I prefer my team work closely, side by side, and so I would need you to temporarily join us in Calgary. That is, you'd be agreeing to move to Canada for a short while to complete the work."

She sucked in her lips, her brows knitting together. In all her planning, Lin hadn't factored in relocation. What he said made sense. He'd likely want to oversee what she was creating and have a say in her designs for his godmother's event. Though she did have in mind negotiating wiggle room for her creative license, she didn't think that mattered right then.

"Canada," she echoed softly.

"Canada," he repeated with his usual blank expression. Familiar but not reassuring.

"I'd have to think about it…" She trailed off when her phone buzzed in her purse. Pulling it out, she stood with the phone in hand and muttered, "Sorry, I have to take this. It's my grand-father."

The call was quick. Her grandfather wanted to know whether she'd be willing to host a last-minute business dinner for some of his col-leagues. It was why she had hesitated to agree to Karl's parameters. Going to Canada meant leaving her grandfather behind to fend for him-self. He was pushing eighty, and though he was fit as a fiddle, he was slowing down. Not to men-tion he'd long since relied on her for day-to-day tasks from housekeeping duties to hosting din-ner parties. Who would tell the chef to prepare his pilau the way he liked it? Who would cohost his work dinners when she left for Canada?

She rubbed her temples as she walked back to their table. Losing her appetite, she picked at her food before pushing her plate away for good.

"If I agree, I will need a week to prepare, at the very least," she said, firm about not budg-ing that deadline. If he thought she was being unreasonable, then she didn't want to work with him.

It was a relief when he agreed. "That's fine. Take two weeks, even. I'll need to file for a rush work permit and prepare a space for you at my office."

His office. It sounded so official already. A skitter of pleasure raced through her as she beamed at him. Some of that pleasure had to do with the rogue twinkle in his darkly mysterious eyes.

She couldn't help teasing him. "Guess I should be glad you accused me of stealing." Awkward though it had been, without it they wouldn't have had the opportunity to meet like this.

Lin didn't expect the atmosphere to change.

She saw him frown, and she frowned too. "What is it?" Was he having second thoughts about working with her already?

"I shouldn't have accused you of stealing." A muscle in his jaw leaped, once, twice. "I'm sorry," he said gruffly, though she inferred the roughness to his tone had more to do with the fact that he wasn't used to apologizing. He didn't seem the sort to admit he'd made a mistake. *Alpha* she'd label him, but not to the point that he had her wanting to hurl a drink into his face. His apology rang as genuine and heartfelt. He was sorry. And she had already figured he'd suffered through some embarrassment for leaping to conclusions.

"You were trying to protect my friend's wedding."

"I could have handled the...*situation* better."

She grinned and leaned in. "I won't disagree there."

He really did smile then. Shocking her into a

breathless state from one heartbeat to the next. He was hot as his intense, brooding self, but he was something else entirely when his lips pulled back and his teeth gleamed brilliantly at her. The only thing that stopped her from drooling madly and babbling incoherently was the waiter choosing that perfect moment to save her with their bill.

But then the universe wrenched the save out of her hands when she and Karl reached for the bill at the same time. Her palm stilled atop his hand, her eyes growing large, and her face hotter than Nairobi's dry seasonal climate. Belatedly she yanked her hand away. By then it was too late. Judging by the way he slowly lifted the bill and plucked his wallet out to pay for their meal and tip the waitstaff and then some, he'd felt the same arresting spark that she had.

Her heart thumped faster in reaction to his heavy look, and her mouth went dry. She was attracted to him, but attraction hadn't ever left her feeling so vulnerable before. Then again, none of her previous boyfriends or dates could ever replicate Karl's naturally hooded eyes, sculpted facial structure, slightly bent nose and pouty brown lips. None of them would have dared to accuse her of stealing a vase, one that belonged to her or otherwise. And not one of them would've inspired her to blush several times in their presence.

She shouldn't indulge her crush on him.

Karl was a good-looking man. Perfect eye candy. But she didn't know him. And if she got to know him, it would be as business partners. She was doing this so she could prove to herself and to her grandfather that forging her own career path was viable. It was the least she could do before he decided to step down and name her as his successor.

Besides, attraction led to attachment, and from there a natural progression to affection…

And love, she thought.

She wasn't ready to fall in love. Not with anyone. More than that, Lin didn't want to tempt love into existence with what felt like a harmless crush on Karl now. She'd have to fight this attraction for him. Snap a lid on it before she signed up to work with him.

Outside the restaurant, Karl flagged a taxi that was parked nearby.

"When's your flight?"

"I have a couple of hours before I have to check out, but there are a few work-related tasks I have to complete before then." He stared down at her, pensively she might even say if she could read his facial expression more easily. "We should exchange numbers. Keep in touch, so I know what your decision will be."

"I know what my decision is," she said, biting back a sigh and punching her number into his phone. "I just have some things to tie up, and then I'm coming to Canada."

"Then, I'll see you in Canada." With a final look, he swiveled on his heels and caught his cab. She watched him until the traffic swallowed him up and he was out of sight. Alone, she walked a few blocks, deep in thought, before her phone buzzed. She perked up when she saw the message was from Karl.

Just making sure you save my number.

Giddier than she ought to feel, she messaged him back.

It's saved now. Have a safe flight.

She sent the text before she could overthink its simplicity.

When her phone vibrated a second time, she nearly dropped it from the hurry to check her messages.

It should be interesting to work with you.

Karl's reply wasn't anything special. He was being polite. She got that. Did it stop her heart from knocking more wildly against her ribs? Nope. Lin pressed the phone to her chest, forcing calming breaths in and out through her nose before giving a little victorious squeal. Then spying a free taxi ahead, she hailed it and gave the driver her home address. She had to speak to her grandfather. The sooner she caught him up to speed about the plan she'd hatched with Karl, the quicker she could book a flight to Canada.

CHAPTER FIVE

Two weeks later

THE SOUND OF rain pelting his office windows
melded with the noise of his fingers clacking
the keyboard. Karl sent the email to a client and
opened another one sitting in his drafts folder.
Only ten more things on my to-do list. That
was what he'd thought an hour ago. Then an
hour had passed. And another. Finally, when he
looked up from his dual computer monitors and
stretched the kinks out of his neck and shoulders, he realized the rain had stopped and the
sky had darkened not from a storm but in night-
fall.

Dusk had quietly slipped through his office.
He hadn't even known when he'd flicked on his
desk lamp to compensate for the loss of gray
daylight. Standing, he took a moment to gaze
out the wide picture window behind his desk.
Snow had fallen intermittently the past few days

with the cold rains he'd grown accustomed to this time of year. The city had one foot in autumn and the other toeing into winter already. But snowstorms were common in October, and there were a couple of days left of September.

He filled his lungs and sighed slowly, as much needing something to do as occupying his mind.

Because tonight wasn't like any other night. In approximately an hour, Lin's flight would be arriving from Europe.

It was tough to admit, but she'd been on his mind since he had last seen her. He accepted the strong attraction he felt for her. On top of that, he noted some similarities between them. He empathized with her plight when it was obvious that she wanted to break free of her grandfather's hold on her. She clearly loved the old man, but she'd have to decide for herself if that love was holding her back. He'd been forced to make a similar decision after his parents had left him with no choice. If they hadn't pushed him out of the proverbial nest, he might never have realized how unhappy he'd been.

She was talented. He'd seen it for himself. It had been enough to impress him into hiring her. It'd be a waste if Lin couldn't see it or do anything about it. But it was neither his journey to take nor his decision to make. The choice was her own.

No matter how much he suddenly wanted to intervene.

On a grudging note, he supposed it was hard to turn one's back on family. At least it appeared that way for her. He was the last person to understand what that felt like. Severing ties with his family had been exactly the thing he'd needed to do to discover himself.

He cleared his mind and then turned to clear his desk. Normally he'd work for long stretches well into the evening, but he'd planned to meet Lin at the airport. She had kept him posted via texts, which was how he knew she'd be arriving shortly, and that cut his time at the office. Karl found he wasn't bothered by the disruption to his schedule. He didn't know what to make of it. Even after he'd had some distance, whenever he thought of Lin his skin seemed to grow all hot and tense. His attraction to her was obvious. But what he couldn't understand was why he was allowing it to affect him as much as it did. It wasn't even like he wanted to date her. He absolutely couldn't, now that she'd be working with him.

That didn't stop his body from reacting so intensely to the merest thought of her.

He'd considered scratching the itch that was building inside him. Dating seriously wasn't something he had done since college.

Since Isaiah.

Isaiah had been his first and only serious lover. They had dated through college after meeting in one of their first-year courses. It had started as a quickly formed friendship. They'd just clicked so perfectly, their values and goals aligning. And then one night in Karl's cramped dorm as they crammed for a final together, Isaiah had kissed him, and he'd found that it felt right. That *they* felt right together. They'd dated through college and even made plans for their future. Plans that included buying their first home together, living out their dreams, supporting each other through good times and bad. Marriage had been mentioned a few times, but they'd been two hopelessly in-love kids. Karl had been happy. He'd met Isaiah's family, and they were exactly the opposite of what he thought families were like. He had only known what *his* parents had been like, what his relationship with *his* siblings had devolved into: bitterness, rivalry, jealousy. With Isaiah and his family, he'd finally gotten to see just how unnaturally cold and loveless his upbringing had been at the hands of his parents.

Just when he thought he could escape it all, when his parents had kicked him out, and he could be with Isaiah just as he had envisioned through their college years, Isaiah pulled the rug out from under him by suggesting they break up.

He'd been gutted then. Torn up about what he'd done wrong.

Isaiah had said he couldn't handle the gloomy person Karl had apparently become after his parents had turned him out of the house.

He closed his eyes and conjured his ex-lover's grim face as he'd said, "You're not the same person I fell in love with. I can't seem to make you happy, and I don't know what will."

Karl snapped his eyes open and gnashed his teeth at the memory and the pain it still caused him.

That was behind him now. The takeaway being that he couldn't be bothered to give love another chance, not when all it had done was hurt him. Moreover, he didn't *need* love. He was a grown man, well into his thirties. He'd gotten used to casual hookups with trusted lovers. Women and men who weren't looking for anything serious, but who also wouldn't use him for his money and business prestige. The last thing he desired was his company's name and his reputation being dragged through the mud for an indiscretion.

He'd been lucky that all his past lovers had been discreet.

He should call one of them soon. But every time

he went to, he would stop shy of going through with it. Something was clearly wrong with him. And he'd remedy it soon as he knew exactly what it was. Karl jutted his jaw as he packed his embossed leather briefcase.

A knock on his office door grabbed his attention.

When he called out for the person to come in, the door opened and his godmother sashayed in, looking as vibrant as the vase of flowers sitting atop his glass-topped coffee table in the seating area of his office. She wore a sunshine-yellow pantsuit under her tangerine wrap coat, her string of polished pearls the only thing that was understated. Even her Moschino purse was loud and cartoonish. Patting her braided updo, she shrugged her shoulders at him and gave the most innocent smile.

"I thought I'd check in on my favorite godson."

"Auntie Carrie," he greeted her, with his jaw just a little harder and that knot of muscles between his shoulder blades more bound up.

He channeled his exasperation into something productive, like walking over to hang up her coat. He knew his godmother too well to relax and treat this like any normal visit. It was never that simple when Carrie dropped in unannounced. She was busy running her own thriving business. Her gift shop kept her preoccupied. It didn't hold her back from nosing into his personal life. If they didn't have the close relationship they did, Karl would have been more exasperated than he was.

If he didn't know he loved her like a mother, he'd have turned her out of his office.

"I'm surprised to see you." He led her to the creamy white leather sofa and grabbed one of the two black velvet barrel chairs across from her.

"Stefon is watching over the shop in my place," she explained breezily. Her retired husband was holding down the fort for them. "I told him he should be resting, but he insists that staying cooped up indoors is doing him in." She threw up her hands and blew a huffy breath. "Men. Stubborn when they're young, and impossible when they're old and graying."

But even as she said it, her eyes softened, and her words held none of the irritation they should. It was how Karl knew she didn't mean anything she said about the love of her life.

Eight months ago, Stefon had had triple by-pass surgery to ward off a second heart attack after the first one had nearly stolen his life. Karl had been there for his godmother. Watched the horror of a near death suck the color and vibrancy out of her. He'd had trouble recognizing her during that time. Trouble understanding how anyone could take that risk with love and then pick up and continue on like it was nothing when the terror passed, and all was right as rain again.

On the one hand, Carrie and her husband were exactly what he'd thought he had once wanted. A marriage, a family and the kind of happiness that was a simple extension of loving and being loved in return. But then he thought of his parents: their marriage was so unlike what Carrie and Stefon had. Charles and Serenity had married as part of a business arrangement. It had been a union of convenience on both sides. A vow of commerce rather than of love. Charles Sinclair was the heir and CEO of a multimillion-dollar construction company; Serenity was the chairperson of her own family legacy in real estate. They were both rare Black business moguls in their respective industries, so it made sense for them to marry and unite their powerful backgrounds.

From the outside it sounded practical. In practice it had been a disaster. They hadn't grown to love each other over that time. Decades together and they still were frosty to one another. In fact, the only time he could recall his parents ever agreeing on something was how they chose to raise their children. Unfortunately his parents believed it was enough putting them into expensive private schools, hiring nannies and tutors, and using their money and public standing to open what they considered were the so-called right doors for Karl and his siblings when they moved onto college and, later, the workforce. Demonstrating concepts to their kids like kindness, decency and love were extraneous to his parents.

He'd known that he didn't want their loveless relationship—not for all the money in the world.

But he also now knew—after all he'd gone through with Isaiah—that he didn't want the kind of love that Carrie and Stefon had either. It was just as equally terrifying to be in a passionless romance as it was to fall so deeply and devastatingly in love that the loss of that love could ruin him forever.

He didn't know how his godmother endured it.

Carrie jarred him back into the present with a little cough and a sly smile. "I believe we have our special guest arriving."

He'd briefed Carrie about Lin. Once his godmother had heard about the unique three-dimensional art Lin could create, she had shown interest in working with her. Just as he'd suspected she would. But even with the excitement she'd displayed, Karl hadn't expected that alone had brought Carrie around to his office, and so late when his team were likely heading out for the day.

"She's flying in, yes." He hoped that would be all. Sorely mistaken, he settled back in his seat when he noted a spark of interest lighting his godmother's eyes. The first sign that she'd only just begun and that his plan to head to the airport to pick Lin up was in danger of being delayed.

"You've been talking on and on about her, it's almost as if I've met her already."

"Considering she'll be here soon, you'll get the opportunity."

Carrie sucked her teeth, cutting his sass off. "That's not what I meant, and you know it."

He curbed an eye roll, knowing that his godmother would only torture him more if he tried it. It left him with no other option than to let her speak her mind and hope that he wasn't affected by whatever it was she had to say.

"You're interested in this Lin."

"I *admire* her designs, and I know they'll be an asset to your event," he stressed the difference, sweating a little more under the collar when his thoughts strayed to Lin and his heart picked up its pace. This was why he didn't want to have this conversation with Carrie, of all people. She was perceptive; she had an uncanny ability to know exactly what he was thinking and feeling.

It had been helpful to him when he had been abandoned by his parents and he was hurting from the breakup with Isaiah. Back then he'd appreciated not having to spell out his pain for Carrie to know how he was feeling. She just did, and she quietly supported him in whatever way he needed. Emotionally and financially, until he'd gotten on his own two feet and his business had taken off.

"You like her," Carrie deadpanned.

"She'll be working with me." It was a moot point. And even if she weren't…

If she weren't, I'd still keep away.

The force of his attraction was enough cause for worry.

So it didn't matter if he had an instant crush on Lin or not. His gut was flashing warning signs, and he had no reason to ignore them. Because love was a door he'd closed and sealed tightly, and no one would get him to open it and try again.

It didn't deter his godmother, though.

"Work romances are a thing, aren't they?" Carrie smirked knowingly.

Karl wasn't winning this, so he stood and tried another tactic. "I should hit the road now if I want to beat traffic."

And before he could hustle her out of his office, she gently tapped a finger to one of the golden-rayed lilies in the floral arrangement decorating his coffee table. They were the only spot of color besides his godmother's attire in his monochromatic workspace. "Flowers. I can't think of anything that could be more welcoming. Imagine what she'll think when you greet her with a beautiful bouquet."

Flowers, he noted subconsciously, liking the idea more than he likely should. Now the question was what kind of flowers were best.

Lin couldn't believe he'd gotten her flowers. She sniffed the spherical yellow and orange flower heads, the thistlelike shape of the petals like nothing she'd ever seen before. Karl opened the door to her apartment and rolled in the last of her bulky designer suitcases. He had told her to wait while he made the return trip and ignored her offer of help. Somehow she found it difficult to disobey him when he spoke so authoritatively.

A frisson of desire crackled through her center, making her more highly aware of him than she'd thought was possible, even when he'd been in Kenya with her. She didn't remember being *this* attracted to him. It was a little more than daunting. And she had enough on her mind as it was. Leaving her grandfather behind had been harder than she'd believed it would be. He hadn't been supportive of her coming to Canada to work with Karl. Then there was the guilt she felt knowing that he'd have to cope without her when he was so used to having her around. She fought the misery off tirelessly through her flight, but now that she had landed safely at her destination, she didn't have the same store of energy to push back against the melancholy breaching her defenses.

"Do you like the flowers?" Karl was looking at her. His question gave her sadness pause.

She loosened the chokehold she had on the bouquet, took another sniff that calmed her frazzled emotions and sighed, smiling. "They're lovely. What are they called?"

"Safflowers. The florist picked them out."

Her smile drooped a little at that, but she perked up, remembering that he'd still made the effort to welcome her to his country and city. It was slowly dawning on her that she had traveled thousands of miles and most of a day to begin this new chapter in her life. And a little more than two weeks after she'd met him. He was taking a chance on her, and she was still a virtual stranger to him.

At least someone believes I can do this.

"Is something the matter?" Karl's deep voice husked over to her from where he was arranging her luggage neatly by the front door. He was staring with such intensity she felt a blush unspool through her body, the heat making her breasts heavier and concentrating between her thighs.

"Nothing. I'm just a little tired from the long flight." She'd flown commercial—first-class, but commercial, nevertheless. Despite knowing that she had free access to her grandfather's jet, she didn't feel right using it after they'd argued their way into a stalemate over her traveling to Canada.

"You're frowning. Is the apartment not to your liking?"

He'd been kind enough to lease a place for the duration of her stay. The luxury apartment was fully furnished, and from what she'd seen of the professional-grade kitchen and the spacious, modern living space, he had her comfort in mind.

"It's perfect. Like the flowers," she said with another whiff of the pleasant display cradled in her arm.

But she sensed that he was still curious, so she divulged some of the truth. In hope that he'd rest easier knowing that she was comfortable in her new home.

"I'm reliving my arguments with my grandfather. He wasn't happy that I was coming here." She didn't mention that he'd also questioned Karl's intentions. Her grandfather wasn't a suspicious man by nature. She knew he was trying to protect her, just as he'd shielded her from feeling the loss of her dad when he'd passed away, and how he didn't mention her mother to her unless she asked. Which she didn't often do because she worried it'd open up buried trauma from having been abandoned by her mom.

"Did you want me to speak to him?" Karl moved closer, a frown that probably matched hers crossing his face. "I could explain to him what you'd be doing here for my company."

As thoughtful as his offer was, it wouldn't do any good. Once her grandfather got an idea into his head, he could be mulish about surrendering it. And he'd long planned for her to take over the family company. As far as he was concerned, nothing should stop that from happening—not even if Lin had told him she had no desire to run his company after he retired.

Shaking her head, she sighed. "It'll only make him dig his heels in more. He can be stubborn—" She winced, hating to talk behind his back. She'd been brought up to respect her elders, but it was hard to do when her grandfather showed little respect for what she loved to do. "Anyways, you won't change his mind about how he views my 3D designing."

"What does he think of it?"

Seeing that Karl seemed to care, she said, "To him, I'm doing a hobby. Something that can't possibly provide for me in the future. He tried to get me to compromise and do my *hobby*—" she said with air quotes "—on the side while he showed me the ropes of taking over his company."

"Does this change our arrangement?"

Blinking in confusion, she frowned anew. "I'm still fully committed to seeing this through, if that's what you're asking."

"Good. Because it'd be a shame to lose your talent. My godmother's excited to meet you too."

Hearing that almost made it worth traveling far from home without the support of the one person she wanted most to back her endeavor. She didn't realize her eyes were watering until her vision blurred.

Quietly, Karl walked away and returned with a tissue in hand.

"Thanks," she mumbled, wiping at her eyes and careful not to jostle the pretty flowers he'd gifted her. "It's just nice *someone* on this end believes in me." She had Machelle, but her best friend hadn't raised her. Her grandfather would always hold a special place in Lin's heart for all the sacrifices he'd made to provide for her when her dad had died and her mom had walked out. He was her only family. And she was worried to death that he'd suddenly stop loving her because of the choice she'd made to come to Canada to work with Karl.

Embarrassment careered through her once she dried her eyes.

Rather than scoffing at her or staring with pity in his intense gaze, Karl said, "Show him what he can't see. The talent and hard work that brought you this far."

"I'll try." She didn't say it with much conviction, though.

He heard it and shook his head. "Make me believe that you mean it."

She breathed slowly and thoughtfully through her nose and then gave it another go.

"I can do it."

"A little better. But it won't cut it because I don't believe it."

Her frustration had been simmering for nearly a day now. All during her flight she'd been wringing her hands, oscillating between being angry at her grandfather and wanting to please him and giving in to his demands. He'd sacrificed for her. Wasn't it time for her to do the same for him, even if it meant her happiness was on the line?

"Make me *believe* you," he stressed, those dark eyes of his cutting through her.

A switch flipped in her, and when she opened her mouth, she didn't recognize the words coming out or the emotion thrumming through her.

"Damn it, I *can* do this! I'm the only one who can do this, and that should be enough."

Lin hadn't felt the quiver in her hands until the bouquet trembled slightly. Somehow Karl had dragged out the fear of losing her grandfather's love and of being abandoned by him and channeled it into strength. She burned with the power of belief in herself. Her head rushed with the sensation, and her heart was fuller for it.

She needn't look to Karl to see his approval.

Though his face barely dropped its cool guard, he was smiling and nodding, and she didn't think that anything else could have made her feel better at that moment. The swooping in her stomach and the breathless tightening in her chest were just products of the outburst she'd just had…or so she told herself. It wasn't because Karl looked sexier smiling, or that she suddenly noticed how close he was to her, his cologne in the air she breathed, and his body heat so enticingly near.

She just had to remember that he was now *technically* her boss…

Making him very forbidden fruit.

CHAPTER SIX

LIN WOKE AND dressed earlier than usual with a fresh confidence the next day.

She had Karl to thank for her good mood.

He'd left her with her hope renewed. She would need the positive thinking if she stood any chance at turning her grandfather on to the idea of her starting a business in 3D designing and printing.

She had a big day ahead, and she didn't want to arrive late. That much she could control. How Karl's staff would react to her was a whole other problem.

I hope they like me.

Otherwise, she was in for a few long months in Canada.

She left her apartment when she received an alert that her ride was waiting downstairs. Karl had told her before leaving yesterday that he'd send a company car to pick her up. The drive itself was short. She was surprised to discover that she didn't live that far from the headquarters.

Once she stepped out of the car, Lin gawked up at the building from the curb. She steeled her spine and focused on the revolving glass doors into the towering monolith of offices. The elevator ride up was quiet and unintrusive. Everyone seemed to have already started their day, which only made her skin feel tighter and itchier and caused her anxiety to spike up again. Her newfound confidence had left the building temporarily, and she hated that it stranded her. She wrapped her arms around her swooping middle, her chest weighty and her mouth drying as she tipped her head up and watched the floors close in on Karl's offices.

His company occupied three whole floors from what the building's security had told her at the front desk when she'd stopped to ask for directions.

It should have comforted her to know that his business was doing just as well as she had hoped. Good for her, because she'd have plenty of work to do and a chance to prove that she could seriously make a profitable career out of her 3D printing. And the best part of it was that she'd have something to show her grandfather by the end of it.

Assuming he was still on speaking terms with her by then.

She sighed and pushed any doubts out of her mind.

The elevator stopped, and the doors opened onto a spacious and welcoming reception center. Its waiting area had a kitchenette, complete with a well-equipped coffee machine and a mini-fridge that she imagined stored an assortment of beverage options for guests. Eyeing one of the plush chairs when she saw the reception desk was unattended, she picked up one of the tablets stacked neatly in a varnished wooden tray, a note on the side inviting guests to surf freely with Wi-Fi-ready technology while they waited.

She'd barely gotten one of the gaming apps open when a familiar voice came from behind her.

"You arrived," Karl said.

She shot up and beamed, hopefully compensating for her nerves. He'd read her easily the last time she spoke to him. She didn't want him thinking that she was wavering in her decision to stay and work with him.

If he noticed her clamoring anxiousness to get her first day started, his expression gave no hint of it. As always he was calm and unperturbed.

He also wasn't alone.

Two women flanked him. Looks-wise, they

were opposites. But their smiles were matched in warmth and friendliness.

Karl made the introductions. "This is Nadine, a senior coordinator and event planner with Heartbeat."

The name was familiar...

Reading her thoughts, Nadine shook her hand and said, "I was the planner working with your friend, Machelle. Unfortunately I couldn't make it to the party in Kenya, but Karl was able to take my place."

Right. That was where she remembered her name from. Machelle had mentioned her before. Nadine was a short and curvy green-eyed red-haired beauty, and her skin was such a fair beige that the brown freckles smattering her cheeks stood out even more. She seemed as sweet as she looked, and Lin felt the anxiety of meeting a new face ease a little.

"Miranda's our capable receptionist. She helps us run this place," Karl said of the other woman.

"You forgot *personal assistant*," Miranda sassed, her perfect teeth flashing as bright as her rich umber skin glowed blemish-free and healthfully. She had her dark brown hair with its honeyed highlights in soft waves, her edges perfectly laid, and her makeup as flawless as her silver jumpsuit, black heels and big hoop earrings.

"Are you volunteering?" Karl snorted, but he

didn't sound or look upset by what she'd said. Lin was surprised. If any of her grandfather's employees had spoken like that to him, they'd have been tossed out on their ear in a flash. The easy camaraderie that obviously existed between Karl and his staff was new to her and nothing she'd ever experience in Kenya. The way she'd been raised, elders in the personal and work spheres were always respected, never talked back to and not treated like they were friends.

It was nice to see that she would be working in a less strict environment. Refreshing, really. She wondered how much of that had to do with wanting to get to know Karl more.

When she'd first met him, she had thought she had gotten a fix on him. He'd seemed cold, unreachable, but intelligent and perceptive. All the traits that likely paved a path to his successful business. In that way he reminded her of her grandfather.

But then he showed glimpses into a more caring nature. And last night he had done plenty for her that she hadn't expected. The flowers, the apartment... It wasn't enough that he'd hired her services and taken a chance on her, he was showing himself to be much kinder than she'd pegged him.

Again, so much like her headstrong grandfather.

With both men, it appeared there was more than met the eye. More beneath their hard, crusty exteriors.

"We should start the tour." Karl extracted himself from the banter with his friendly staff and moved to call the elevator. "Your workspace is on the floor below these offices."

She wouldn't be working near him. Why did that knowledge deflate her mood?

Nadine and Miranda waved goodbye as Lin joined Karl in the elevator. She didn't have long to fidget by his side in the thick, unnerving silence. The ride was short, and before long she was too distracted by her new view to be entranced by the spiced fragrance of his cologne and the minty smell of his aftershave or body wash.

"Wow," she heard herself say breathily.

She was speechless when Karl led her off the elevator into a vast, open-spaced studio. Tall concrete pillars, exposed brick walls and bright, shiny hardwood flooring popped out at her first. Then she noticed the work benches, six of them evenly dispersed. A lounge and kitchenette area that were glassed off. She spied a large flat-screen TV in the lounge, along with a comfy-looking seating space to kick back and relax.

But what really had her jaw dropping to the

point she worried she'd have to pick it up from the floor with both her hands was the printers.

She counted six in total, one for each workbench.

Two were large-scale printers that she knew for a fact had to have cost tens of thousands each. All printers were fully assembled, and she figured ready to begin printing if a file were extruded and delivered to them.

She finally managed an awe-filled "Wow!"

"We can rework any areas you're unhappy with. Feel free to let us know what you'd like and need to complete your designs."

Lin goggled at him, trying to gauge whether he was for real. When she realized that he was being dead serious, she snorted, slapped a hand over her mouth and then released the laughter that had quickly built up. She muffled most of it with her hand, but she saw his brows snap up at the noise that slipped free.

"I'm sorry. It's just I can't see how this—" she waved her hands around them at the studio space he'd recreated for her purposes "—could get any better."

"You're pleased," he commented, his thicker, darker eyebrows lowering from their defensive posturing.

"More than pleased," she said a little too hurriedly, and for a moment she didn't recognize who she was, because it sounded like she was flirting. Her voice pitched higher, and the playful note in her response was as clear as the bright day shining through the expansive row of sash windows that took up an entire wall of the floor.

Karl moved nearer to a window, his hands slipping into his trouser pockets, and his back briefly to her before she trailed him to where he stood. She was taken aback when the natural lighting to the room draped him. He was droolworthy standing in the shaft of white sunlight. His bald head gleaming, his shirtsleeves rolled up, forearms taut with lean, clean muscle, his dark brown skin contrasting against his softlooking cotton oxford shirt and his top buttons undone so casually it had her mouth dry and her heart rate picking up concerningly.

He turned his face to the light, the squint to his eyes adding a realness to his otherwise ethereal beauty. He could be on a magazine cover. With his height and slim but trim build, a fashionrunway model. But his job was still glamorous. Heartbeat Events wasn't a struggling event company in a saturated market with plenty of competition. The clients Karl and his staff worked with and created unforgettable events and experiences for were the crème de la crème of society. Multimillionaire moguls, A-list actors, top-charting musicians, popular politicians—she could probably name just about anyone wealthy and well-known, and he'd likely have had the chance to provide them with his company's services.

There was a reason she'd decided to work with him. If she was going to put everything on the line, it would be because she'd bargained on the power of his success rubbing off on her.

"Are you good to continue?"

She nodded and followed him as he walked her through her new workspace. It was hard to believe that he'd done all of this to make her feel comfortable. And in so short a time. Only two weeks had passed since he'd requested she work alongside his team in Canada. He'd managed all of this in that time and with what little input he had asked of her. He no doubt had done his share of research in what she needed to complete her 3D projects.

He must have also been paying attention back in my studio.

She recalled him observing her workspace in Kenya and showing interest that had her sparkling all over even now as she reminisced.

Concluding the tour, Karl guided her back to the elevator. "I have your work permit and some paperwork for you to fill out in my office. After that, I thought it'd be a good idea to introduce you to my godmother. She's expecting us."

"She is?" Anxiety gripped her. This was it. She

was doing this work for him to please his god-mother. If she failed to do that, she'd have wasted her time and effort, and her dream to be her own boss would be that much more out of reach.

"I mentioned yesterday that she's been look-ing forward to meeting you. She owns a gift shop not too far from here."

A fellow entrepreneur. Lin didn't know why that was a bit calming. At least she now knew she was in good company. Maybe they'd even have something to talk about besides the event Karl was planning for his godmother. She could only hope.

Karl had been thinking about how to mitigate the effect Carrie might have on Lin when they first meet. It didn't help that his godmother had gotten it into her mind that there was something going on between him and Lin. When in fact what Carrie had sensed was his desire for Lin and his hyperawareness of her whenever she was in his thoughts or in physical proximity.

He wasn't about to confess to his attraction.

It would give Carrie a strong reason to play at matchmaker. And *that* wasn't something he could have happen.

This partnership with Lin wasn't about that. He had closed his heart off to anything more than no-string flings with partners who were of the same noncommitment mindset. And even if he entertained asking Lin if she were interested in hooking up, what mattered now was they were working together. Pleasure and business never mixed very well. He'd seen it with his parents. They were so busy running and managing their real estate and construction business that they never considered what their loveless marriage had done to their family, to their children.

To me, he thought grimly.

It was all the more reason not to fall for the lure of his lustful thoughts and emotions and to strictly draw a professional line where Lin was concerned.

The charming silver bell above the shop's front door dinged when he strolled in with Lin.

Her eyes went round, her head turning this way and that.

Karl tried to see it from her perspective. There was an old-timey appeal to his godmother's shop, The Gift Goddess. Gleaming wood-paneled walls and hardwood flooring that was varnished dark and polished to perfection. Handmade shelves and a long glass display case beside the front service desk.

Lin picked up a ceramic ashtray with a silhouette of a beaver painted inside and on the back.

She paused to read the small note where she'd lifted the ashtray from and looked adorable with her brows knitted together in concentration.

"Local artisans made everything you see. They use locally sourced material and sell to my godmother." It had been an ingenious business idea when his godmother opened the store more than fifteen years ago. Calgary was a lively metropolis, and in recent years it had become a hot spot for tourists from all over the country and the world. Though, it hadn't always been a sprawling concrete jungle. Like most other places in Canada, it had history, and that history had appealed to his godmother enough for her to connect her vision of business with her love of art.

That clever merger was what had opened the doors of The Gift Goddess. A gift shop that allowed tourists to take a piece of their memories of Calgary with them in the form of locally made pieces. And there was something for everyone. Postcards and key chains, T-shirts and caps, belt buckles, cowboy boots, photography and oil paintings. Carrie was always outsourcing, discovering new artists and new art mediums. One time she'd sold handmade traditional wooden snowshoes. It was her zeal and penchant for business that had kept the shop running all these years.

It's why Carrie had inspired him to kick-start his own business.

She believed that his parents played a role too, but he wasn't anything like them. If they had given him one thing, it might have been his business savvy. Not that he was rushing to concede that fact. The less he thought of his parents and the less he had to do with them, the happier he was.

Lin set down the ashtray and moved around the store with riveted attention, checking out as many items as she could.

Her fascination came to an end when Stefon and Carrie walked out from the backroom. They were arguing about Stefon carrying a hefty-looking box. Carrie sounded as worried as she was annoyed that her husband was ignoring her and doing all the heavy lifting.

"The doctor warned you to take it easy." She swatted Stefon's back, grumbling, "Why are you being so pigheaded?"

"Yeah, well, what the doc doesn't know won't hurt."

She huffed at his response, unamused.

Stefon set down the box and then turned to bundle his wife into his arms. He was short and stout, and his short curly hair was entirely gray, but he cleaned up nicely with his typical sweater-and-jeans combo.

"Forgive me," he said after a kiss to her forehead.

She swatted his shoulder this time, but without the same vehemence, the smile on her face softer, more loving.

Before they continued, Karl coughed to grab their attention.

They pulled apart at the sight of them. His godmother patted the sides of her African-print headscarf, looking resplendent in a dress that matched the scarf's print. She was uniquely vibrant as usual, but he imagined that Lin might be taken aback by Carrie's style.

So it was surprising when Lin sprung in with a question. "Do you sell Ankara dresses?"

They struck up conversation like that. No formal introductions. Just straight into an appreciation of African fashion and design.

At one point, Stefon sidled up beside him.

"Is that her? The woman Carrie says you've been talking on and on about?"

"Yeah, that's her." Karl didn't correct him about the rest of it. He was too mesmerized by Lin's smiles and laughter at whatever Carrie was telling her. She hadn't smiled or laughed that openly around him yet. It had him wondering what it would take to get her to smile at him like that.

He didn't have to wait long to find out.

When they left Carrie's gift shop, Karl decided not to head back to the office and suggested that they visit a nearby park. He'd sold it as a good place to see the city skyline. But Lin appeared on board whether that was true or not.

Though it was true, and Calgary's downtown skyline was more alluring today with a cloudless blue sky as the backdrop of its skyscrapers. She gasped at the colorful autumn leaves on the trees in the park, exclaiming with a smile, "They're gorgeous! Like something out of a painting or a dream."

The smile was what got him. He warmed all over, the mild chill in the air blasted away at the first blush of pride. He'd put that happy expression on her face. And there was this primal urge in him to beat his chest about it. An action he had never thought about doing before.

He had been doing and saying a lot of uncharacteristic things. Like when he spied a perfectly shaped leaf on their path and Lin continued ahead of him, clueless when he stooped to pick it up for her.

"It's got all the colors mixed together," she said of the leaf when he handed it to her.

She was right. The red, yellow and orange blended harmoniously in the leaf. It was a good sign that he'd chosen right and followed his instinct to prolong their time together. Bringing her to enjoy the colours was a good cover for what he'd actually wanted: time alone with her.

Time that he shouldn't really desire.

It was like he was tempting fate, and fate would hit back any moment and make him do something stupid to ruin their work relationship before it had even truly begun.

Just as he thought it, his hand bumped hers and her eyes sprung up to him at the same time as he looked at her. They paused in the middle of the path, gazing at each other. For the first time, he experienced close to the same level of yearning he felt for her mirrored in her eyes.

He opened his mouth, unsure of what he'd say, only knowing that he had to say something. Anything. Because it didn't feel real to him.

"Lin…"

He'd barely said her name when a bike bell chimed ahead in warning, and the moment was lost when they stepped aside out of harm's way.

"Were you saying something?" she asked him a short while later when they continued walking.

He pressed his lips together and shook his head. It didn't feel right taking them back there now.

Lin shrugged and moved on. "I'll have to come to this park again. Maybe jog here or just go for a walk." She lowered her phone, having snapped a photo of the skyline from their hilltop vantage point.

"You better get it in soon. We've had our first snowfall of the season already, and even though it's melted now, the snow will be back soon." It wasn't rare in Calgary to see snow this early. They hadn't gotten through many Octobers without seeing some of the white stuff. They'd even had the occasional drearily white Thanksgiving. Not that it had deterred the leaves from taking their time changing colors. She'd arrived at a good time to see the full glow of oranges, yellows and reds melding together in perfect harmony. Sometimes together on one tree, and sometimes all on one leaf. Like the special leaf she was holding.

"I liked meeting Carrie and Stefon. They seem really sweet."

Lin grabbed an empty bench that faced the pleasant view of his city below.

"That's because they were showing you their best side." He smothered the full effect of his teasing grin. It felt unfamiliar on his face. He was used to acting more reserved around people he didn't know, and he hadn't known Lin for long. But she made him want to laugh and smile almost as much as she had done with his godmother.

Having grown used to bottling his emotions, it wasn't an altogether easy feeling...

But it's not unpleasant either.

A part of him could even see himself getting used to and growing to find comfort in it.

She stroked the leaf he'd given her and sighed. "It's sad what happened to Stefon. Carrie must have had it rough while he was sick."

Karl was still shocked his godmother had told Lin about Stefon's heart attack and subsequent emergency surgery, not to mention the year-long battle of his physical recovery. Every day Stefon looked and sounded more like himself, but it had been a long and tough road Carrie had endured with her husband and family. If Karl hadn't watched it unfold, he wouldn't have known just how challenging it had been on their family and their long-standing love.

Even someone like him who trod carefully around the subject knew what love was when he saw it, and Carrie and Stefon loved each other deeply.

It didn't change his mind about it. Facts were just facts.

Love could heal and empower—and it could just as easily weaken and destroy.

"They had family support."

"You helped them too." She didn't phrase it as a question, assuming that he had been there.

The assumption was correct. "Yes, I helped whenever I could. As did their grown children." He'd run errands whenever one of Carrie and Stefon's kids couldn't do it themselves. Unlike their adult children who had families, Karl was a bachelor with no ties. He didn't have the same family demands that pressed his time. So he had worked particularly hard to free his schedule and delegate more tasks to his staff in order to be there for Carrie and Stefon if and when they needed him.

"It must have been especially tough on Carrie. Their love was clearly strong enough to withstand it."

He grunted by way of agreement, suddenly cagier now that they were discussing love and relationships.

"Have you ever wondered what a love that powerful could feel like?" she asked, her eyes searching ahead, gaze distant.

Karl stared at her, first because the question caught him off guard, and then to take in the way a coil of her hair had slipped free of the butterfly clip she'd used to hold it back from her face. Sunlight highlighted the warmer brown tones in her hair and the red undertone of her brown skin and brightened the glow of her full, sleekly polished lips. Lips he wanted to taste so desperately in that instant, he'd have done it if she didn't blink and look at him with widened eyes.

"I'm sorry! You don't have to answer that. I was thinking aloud."

She *had* asked a personal question that he normally would've evaded. But there was something about talking to her that made it impossible to refuse her. It could have been his reptilian brain doing the talking. Her pretty face making him into an idiot. Yet he knew it wasn't that, but more like a fast and easy trust in her to protect whatever he told her.

She had also been admirably vulnerable with him. Sharing her struggle in differences with her grandfather and seeming to be open to his advice about how to cope.

He couldn't see any harm in replying. "I haven't."

The silence that came after that was charged. They stared at each other for who knew how long before one of them blinked.

But she spoke first. "Should we head back?"

Reluctantly he agreed. He'd had enough alone time with her to last him.

So why do I feel like I want more?

More than they'd had already… Maybe even more than the few months that were left until Carrie's vow renewal and Lin's departure to her home in Nairobi.

CHAPTER SEVEN

LIN'S FIRST WEEK passed by in a blur of activity. She was thinking further ahead than what was in front of her. One she finished rendering one design, she was designing and prepping the printers to print another. Before long she had the stockroom filled with designs that were ready for his godmother's vow-renewal ceremony in a couple of months. But she still had more to do.

By the time she left the office and reached her temporary home in the swanky apartment Karl had leased for her, her whole body was mush, but her spirit and mind were active with ideas for the next day. There was even an evening or two where she'd pulled a near all-nighter to get the ideas she had in her head down on the page so she wouldn't forget them.

Karl expected updates every start of the week at his staffwide brief meetings. She'd kept him abreast of all the work she'd completed during these meetings. But the Monday of the second week was Canadian Thanksgiving, a holiday she had heard of in passing. Still a holiday meant the whole office was closed. Everyone at home celebrating with family or enjoying the free time off work.

Everyone but her.

She had gotten permission from Karl to work. It had happened over a short series of texts. She hadn't missed the fact that they hadn't spoken outside of work since the day they'd visited Carrie's gift shop and the downtown park nearby. Lin hadn't been able to free herself of the niggling sense that he was avoiding her. And if he wasn't avoiding her, then maybe he was treating her as she ought to treat him. Coolly, professionally, and with none of the heat she'd feel whenever he was close to her.

Sighing, she focused on the latest design on her computer screen. It was for a seven-branched candelabra. She'd gotten the idea after doing research on Kwanzaa on her own time. What she learned was that seven candles were lit to represent the seven days of the holiday. A candle for each day until all candles were glowing on the final night of Kwanzaa. Lin had fiddled with the design of the traditional wooden candleholder, or *kinara* as it was called in Swahili. She'd found it interesting that one of her first languages was the language used in Kwanzaa. It seemed fated that she should work on this project and that she should help Karl bring his godmother's vision to life for her event.

Thinking of it that way made her decision feel like it was destined. But it didn't erode her guilt entirely. She hadn't wanted to leave her grandfather, and she hated that he was too stubborn to see that she was happy doing what she was doing.

Lin wiped at her eyes hastily, feeling the tears before they blurred her vision completely.

She walked away from her computer and prepared coffee for herself in the break room. The coffee would jolt new life into her. She wanted to work as long as possible and avoid going home with her sullen thoughts for company.

Lin wasn't paying attention. She'd drifted off waiting for the coffee, the sound of her printers drowning out all other noise.

The noisy printers were why she missed the sound of the elevator pinging open.

And how she didn't notice she was no longer alone in the spacious workroom.

"Lin."

She startled and spun to answer to her name, her heart rate still through the roof when she saw it was Karl. When her nerves faded, though, all she felt was a giddiness to have him close after she'd been thinking of him.

Despite feeling as though he were avoiding

her, she didn't feel any less of the usual heat that engulfed her whole body whenever he was nearby. She blushed from head to toe, her skin hot and achy with a deep primal need. She desired him, and if she weren't careful she'd make it obvious to him now.

Like when she breathed his name, "Karl," and it came out all low and bedroom sexy. With a cough, she raised her voice and added, "What are you doing here?"

He was also the last person she would've expected.

"Sorry if I frightened you." He held up the reusable bags in his hands. "Gifts from Carrie. She insisted I bring them to you. I tried calling."

Lin glanced over at where her phone lay hooked up to a portable charger and on mute as she'd wanted no distractions.

"If you're taking a break, why not break for a quick meal? I can have some of this reheated for you in a flash."

She was still too shocked to see him to argue. It was as though her thoughts had conjured him. Either way, it was hard to look any place else while he navigated the dishes Carrie had given him and set up the microwave to reheat all of it.

When he turned, their eyes locked.

He looked good in his dress shirt and black slacks. His long overcoat hung open, and he had his hands tucked in his coat pockets. He could have stepped out of a magazine or off a runaway. If she weren't careful, she'd be salivating…and she could use the food as an excuse, but deep down she would know the real reason.

Stop before he thinks you're over the top.

The warning came right as he said, "I still don't understand why you didn't take the day off. Carrie thought I left you behind. She wouldn't believe that you'd declined her offer to dinner."

She had thought it was too generous of his godmother to have invited her in the first place. Lin knew that Carrie had only worried like any mother might have. But she hadn't wanted to latch onto her sympathy and intrude on a private family gathering.

Besides, Karl would've been there, and nothing would have been more awkward than spending the holiday with her boss.

Her *very handsome* boss.

She swallowed thickly and moved the conversation along. "Did you enjoy dinner at Carrie's?"

When she'd asked if she could come in to work over the holiday and he'd approved, he had also told her that she could reach him if she needed him at any time. It was thoughtful of him to think of her when he'd been busy celebrating the turkey-focused holiday with Carrie and her family.

"It was eventful." He paused and eyed the cup of coffee in her hands. "Have you been working the whole time?"

"I lost track of how long I've been here." But she'd gotten a lot more work completed because of it. Getting her head down and forgetting her problems and worries had worked for her. Now that her head was raised, and she wasn't alone, she was back to being concerned about the factors in her plan she couldn't control. Like her grandfather...*and* her confusing but exciting feelings for Karl.

The microwave pinged.

Karl grabbed plates from the top cabinets. He'd stocked the break room with everything he could possibly need. Again, his thoughtfulness was at odds with his sometimes-brusque personality.

She helped carry the dinner Carrie had sent over with him to an empty workbench and drooled for real at the mouthwatering spread. Baked mac and cheese, glazed turkey slices, candied yams and buttermilk biscuits. There was even dessert, chocolate pecan pie. Just as she was about to dig in, she noticed Karl standing and watching her.

"I can't eat this all on my own."

He shrugged. "Believe me when I say that Carrie made sure I was as stuffed as her turkey before I left her place. She was also explicitly clear when she said all of this was yours."

Lin gawped at the food that could feed her for days and maybe all of next week.

"At least sit with me while I'm eating." It was a compromise.

He grabbed the stool beside her and continued staring at her.

If she weren't so hungry, she'd have squirmed under his watchful eyes.

"Please tell me you've been eating properly."

"I had lunch earlier."

Much earlier.

"Why do I find that hard to believe?" He breathed deeply through his nose, his eyebrows dipping down. "So why don't you show me what had you so preoccupied that you forgot to eat."

He'd seen right through her. Blushing, she tipped her chin toward her laptop, and he brought it back to his stool, scrolling through the files she had open. They were designs she hadn't gotten to yet. Designs she'd wanted to have him approve. It was another good reason he was here.

"Is this a *kinara*?" He was on the file she'd been tweaking with the Kwanzaa candleholder. Without prompting, he nodded satisfyingly. "It looks good. Carrie will like it." He continued scrolling, the same affirming nod given to each file. Her chest puffed out, and her face was hurting from how big she was smiling.

While he perused her designs, he asked, "Why work today of all days?"

"Why not?" She grabbed a warm biscuit, the scent of it calling to her. "Besides, I'm new to the city."

"My point exactly. I know most retail spots are closed for the day, but you could have explored."

"Are you judging me? I thought you'd be the first person to appreciate my display of strong work ethic. Miranda says you work odd hours all the time." She mumbled the last part around a mouthful of the baked good.

"Should I be worried you two are thick as thieves now?"

Lin laughed, and Karl surprised her when he chuckled low, roughly and sexily. She pressed her thighs together, suddenly feeling a little hotter and wondering whether it'd be too obvious to get up and adjust the thermostat.

Nervous that he'd notice the change in her, she blurted, "Do you go to Carrie's often?"

"Most major holidays. Thanksgiving. Christmas. New Year's. Unless I have plans of my own."

Of course. He was too good-looking to be alone. Women probably threw themselves at him. And maybe one of those women were lucky enough to be his girlfriend. Miranda had said he was private about his life and that no one knew whether he was single or not, but it didn't mean that he was a bachelor. She didn't know why that made her so strangely sad.

She had a crush on him; it didn't mean she planned to do anything about it.

He was her boss. And even when she did complete her job and they went their separate ways, from her experience she hadn't found anything special or worth truly pursuing with any of the people she'd dated. She was too busy to be chasing after a crush and the exquisite high that it gave her being near him. What happened when she came crashing down to reality? There was too much on the line for her to risk. Her grandfather was already upset with her. If she returned home having made Karl's godmother happy, at least she'd feel good about one thing. There was also still hope that her grandfather would give her plan to start a business a chance.

Then there was the fact that Karl might see her differently if they became more than work colleagues. Up till now he'd been unexpectedly kind to her.

That could change if they got all hot and personal...

And he might not be so kind after.

Lin thought of how her mom had stopped loving them and how that had left her dad to

raise her alone—until he'd passed away. The
tightness in her throat and the flash of watery
heat around her eyes reminded her where she
was and with whom. Crying in front of Karl
wasn't an option. He'd ask her questions, and
she wasn't sure she'd be able to keep her face
straight while she lied about the parts of herself
she wasn't ready to share with anyone.

"So you usually stay in the city for the holidays.
What about your family? Do they live here too?"

He kept his face neutral in spite of his heart
beating faster. Talking about his family always
had the same effect on him. He felt restless. Like
he needed to jog a mile or two.

Or ten, he thought grumpily.

"They live in Toronto," he said.

She tipped her head. "Isn't that far?"

What he wished to say was that it wasn't far
enough sometimes. It was like he could still feel
them breathing down his neck. The odd sensation only intensified when he'd understood that
Carrie had invited his parents to her vow renewal. It would be pointless to deny that he had
repressed his feelings about what had happened.

"They'll be here for Carrie and Stefon's event."
They hadn't RSVPed officially, but he'd be prepared if they showed up. This time he would be
wielding power and controlling their fate. He'd

promised Carrie he'd behave. But if his parents so much as stepped a toe out of line with him…

I'll happily walk them out of the party myself.

He ground his teeth, eager to stop thinking about his family as soon as possible.

Lin must have sensed he didn't want to talk about them. She ate in silence for a while before she spoke again.

"I didn't answer you honestly before."

Karl rose above his own thoughts and feelings when he heard her. "About?"

"Why I've chosen to work rather than taking time off on a holiday." She patted her mouth with a napkin, sighed and faced him. "I was feeling lonely, and work helped take my mind off the fact that I'm here alone. Something about it being a holiday and knowing that everyone else is with their family."

She was lonely? Why hadn't she said anything to him about it?

Keeping his voice calm, he asked, "Is there something I can do to help?"

Lin smiled so brilliantly then. "You already have." She gestured to the food, teasing, "Saved me from loneliness and hunger."

He blushed…and the sensation was oddly new but familiar. He hadn't felt like this in a long while, again not since Isaiah broke up with him. Every one of his previous lovers since then hadn't roused this carnal hunger to be closer to someone. To know them so intimately. To feel with the whole of his being that he could trust them with every part of him.

Lin had accomplished that in, what, three weeks of knowing her?

Her hand alighted on his arm. "Thanks for coming to visit and for staying with me."

"It was my pleasure," he answered gruffly, his emotion betraying him.

But if she noticed, her smile posed no judgment of him.

"I was being serious when I said you could call me if you need anything." He'd said it just as nervously the first time too. "If you're ever feeling alone…"

She squeezed and patted his arm. "I'll call you," she said, completing his thought.

Silently he added, *I promise you won't feel lonely again.*

He didn't want to unpack why it was important to him that she felt like she had someone in her corner—only that he wanted her to know that he was here for her while she worked with him. As a colleague. As a confidant.

Never a lover.

But maybe…maybe he could be a friend to her too.

CHAPTER EIGHT

KARL KEPT HIS WORD.

Five more weeks passed, and Lin hadn't felt lonely again. She hadn't even needed to call him. He was just always there, checking in on her, dropping in unannounced on top of the office's weekly meetings. She'd almost say that he was giving her extra-special treatment, and instead of feeling embarrassed that she was being singled out she was touched by his kindness. It also wasn't helping cure her of her crush on him. Discovering all his good traits was making him more attractive to her.

But she was determined to keep from shaking up their cheerful dynamic. They were working together, but these days he almost felt like a friend to her.

When she'd initially met him, Lin didn't think she'd ever call Karl a friend.

He was so unlike her at first glance. *Coolly distant and impersonal* wasn't how she would describe herself. But it had taken a short time to get to see that he had a warmly sensitive center beneath the bland expression he wore too often. Why else would he have been trying to get to know her outside the office?

On top of checking on her, he'd gone above and beyond by showing her the places he liked best in his home city. Almost every evening that she wasn't spending time with Miranda and Nadine, she was with Karl.

It had become such a habit to go out with him that she began showing up to his office when he worked later than the time they were supposed to meet up. This happened rarely, but it was beginning to happen more often in the last week alone, and Lin suspected the reason had to do with it being nearly mid-November and his godmother's Kwanzaa-themed vow renewal gaining on them.

Once she had him out of the office and it was just the two of them, Lin didn't hesitate to ask.

"You're working late again. Is it for your godmother's event?"

He nodded, the weariness in his face intensifying. "Carrie's thinking of changing venues. Of course she asks for it at the last minute to drive me crazy..." He mumbled the last part.

She had to hide her smile and smother her giggle.

"Why doesn't the current venue work for her?" Carrie and Stefon had chosen a lovely heritage home right in the heart of Calgary. Apparently, it had been where they had gone for their first date decades ago, and they'd wanted to relive the experience. Lin had thought it romantic.

"I'll show you what changed her mind." He pulled out his phone and scrolled through photos on his event company's official website. "A couple had a wedding this past summer at a lake resort."

Lin gaped at the image of the picturesque mountain lake that he showed her. She didn't think a lake could be so blue. The snow-capped mountains in the backdrop were majestic. She knew the Rockies were a unique geological formation, but… "They remind me of the mountains of Switzerland. I can see why Carrie would want to change venues."

"I grudgingly agree. But I still had to actually do the work, and I reached out to a friend who manages the resort. Thankfully, they can squeeze us in. I don't think everyone will want to travel the two hours to the location, but that's a hurdle for tomorrow."

She nodded in agreement. He looked too wiped out to do any more work. Selfishly she also didn't want him breaking their plans.

They were eating dinner together. She didn't

have a clue where exactly they were headed, but she figured it had to be within walking distance as he hadn't suggested taking his truck. There had been a few times where he'd taken her to places farther than downtown. Mini golf in a quiet and quaint suburb outside Calgary. A bar and grill off the highway with a view of the city like the one in the park all those weeks ago. Her favorite had been the downhill-karting not too far from where she lived. She hadn't thought she was competitive until she was behind the wheel, ramming Karl off-course. Lin smiled at all the memories he'd given her. She'd have a piece of him always, even when she'd completed her work here and returned home.

"So are you going to tell me where we're going tonight?"

He shook his head, his bald head hidden under a brown knit hat that he'd told her was a gift from Carrie. His black scarf was tied loosely, and his coat was undone, revealing the three-piece suit he'd worn to the office today. Each of his tailored suits had her drooling over him even more, if that were even possible. The luxurious fabrics always molded to his body and show-cased his lean, muscled frame. The long coat and winter gear hid some of that, but oodles of snow on the ground made the air they breathed mist before their faces and sting the tip of her nose and her cheeks.

She curled her fingers together beneath the faux-fur muff that Karl had bought her. The gift had been a surprise. He'd explained that she wasn't dressed to withstand the bitter Canadian cold. She had thought he was exaggerating until she'd gotten a taste of the first snowfall. One day it was autumn, the leaves on the trees a stunning array of golden yellows to ruby reds, and then the next a blizzard dumped several feet of snow over the whole city. Even the trees hadn't been given notice, the fall foliage clinging on stubbornly.

As they walked the streets, she craned her head up slightly to admire the contrast of the damp and browning autumn leaves against the stark colorless snow.

Her attention shifted to the sky-high building they were approaching. The Calgary Tower. Lin had seen it plenty of times from outside, and she wondered when she'd get the time to visit the landmark.

A thought struck her.

"Wait. Are we going up there?"

Karl's small secretive smile told her what she suspected.

"Why didn't you tell me?" She swatted his arm

before giving him a squeeze and the biggest grin. "I told you I wanted to visit the Tower."

"They have the restaurant *and* the view up there, so I was being practical."

Practical was one thing; being sweet was another. Flutters of excitement rippled through her. She looked up at the ginormous building ahead of them, the kaleidoscope of colors lighting the solid spire, a beacon beckoning them closer. She was thrilled to get to see it finally.

Or am I just happy because Karl's with me?

She conceded that it was a bit of both. Lin liked spending time with him. Even if she shouldn't be indulging this crush that she had on him. Giving in to her desire would be disastrous. They still had a professional relationship, and she didn't want to jeopardize the opportunity he'd given her. It didn't matter that she still doubted that any of this would warm her grandfather to the idea of letting her pursue her dream to run her own business.

She pushed aside her troubles and gave in to the experience of visiting the Calgary Tower. The ride up to the restaurant was as quiet as the lobby and gift shop had been. Given how busy the city could be in the evening—even on a weeknight—she was taken aback.

"Is it always this empty?" She looked up at him, the lights of the elevator and the glow of the touchscreen elevator panel illuminating his gorgeous face. Her heart fluttered again.

"It's off-season for tourists, but yes, you'll have noticed that we almost have the place to ourselves."

Almost included the waitstaff that seated them once they entered the impressive restaurant with its panoramic view of the city.

"Where is everyone?"

The restaurant was eerily empty. No other guests were present, and she knew that it couldn't be some coincidence that they were dining alone together. Just the two of them.

She steadfastly ignored her skipping delight at the thought.

Without batting an eye, he said, "I rented the building out for the evening."

She knew that he was flush with money—millions if she factored the success of his business. But it was extravagant and a little unlike him to use his wealth to separate them from the masses. He didn't seem the sort to flash his cash. Sure, she'd noted his designer clothing, his platinum, crystal and gold watches, and his leather shoes and flashy kicks, but he wore them in an understated way that had never looked ostentatious. And she was positive that he lived in some McMansion that rivaled her grandfather's gated sprawling manor, yet he hadn't once made it obvious that he was a millionaire. Several times over.

Those zeros in his net worth hadn't inflated his head. She liked that he was as sensible as she'd been raised to be. The money wouldn't have attracted her to him, anyways. She had plenty of it. Lin liked what she saw, and she liked who he was even more.

Still, she couldn't help but tease him about it. "Did you want me all to yourself?"

"That's a perk too." She heard the mirth in his voice and grasped that he was joking too, but the flame in his hooded eyes arrested her. A desire she recognized as her own mirrored back to her from his side of the table. Under the table, his foot brushed hers, and that small touch ignited a harrowing heat in her lower belly. The flutters she'd been feeling were full-on waves of sensation. She buzzed with the headiness of her yearning for him by the time their first course arrived.

And even when his face reverted to its usual inscrutable mask, she knew what she saw was real.

He wanted her too.

What was he doing?

Karl berated himself through the whole of their meal. He'd been doing well—*fantastic* when he considered that he hadn't made a move on her or made an ass out of himself yet. They had gone out together a few times. All platonic, friendly dates. And all in an effort to keep her from feeling the loneliness that she'd admitted to back at Thanksgiving. He hadn't wanted her to feel the absence of her home while she was doing him a favor. Sure, he was paying her to do the work. He also planned to give her any referrals and help boost her through his own network of clients. Lin and her three-dimensional designs would be popular with a lot of them. She could easily open a business right in the city and do well. But he could indulge the thought no more than he could fantasize about what it'd be like if they were on a romantic date instead.

He hid his scowl behind a glass of red wine.

She sipped at her own nonalcoholic beverage. Since she was Muslim, he had been mindful of her dietary choices. All a part of making her comfortable in his world. He hoped that his efforts hadn't been in vain.

"Would you accompany me to the observation deck?" He stood and held a hand down to her at the culmination of their meal.

She followed his lead, her hand steady in the crook of his elbow.

They took the stairs down to the deck below. She marveled at the golden string of lights circling the whole perimeter. Wordlessly, she looked up at him with a question in her eyes as to whether the presentation of lights was his doing.

He didn't answer her, but he had asked that the place be decorated prettily. This was her first time seeing Calgary from this height. He wanted it to be special for her. Doubly so because he still recalled how nervous and uncertain she'd been when she had first arrived. To think that he might have lost her to her doubt. Things would be different if she'd chosen to turn around and hop on the next flight back to Kenya.

It occurred to Karl that he hadn't told her that it mattered to him that she hadn't left.

Once he found a good spot for her by the only table and stools, he spoke up.

"I'm happy you're here."

"I am too," she said with a quick glance at him before looking away, utterly absorbed by the view. It had been the same revolving nighttime panorama of the city during the whole of their meal, but Lin looked out at the slowly changing vista as though she were seeing it through a brand-new perspective. And though he had *definitely* been to the Calgary Tower before and hosted a few events right there on the observation deck, it had been a refreshing experience to live vicariously through her for the evening.

"That's not what I meant. I'm glad you decided to stay with us."

Lin spared him more than a glance now. "You helped make the decision easier."

He had? "How?" he blurted, intrigued.

"You believed in me being able to do this before I believed in myself."

Karl was surprised that she'd ever doubted herself. He didn't think that he'd played a role, but she was looking at him with such openness, he knew that she wasn't gassing him up just because he was her boss, temporarily or otherwise.

"It's been hard, though, I'll admit. I've had days where I can't stop thinking about what awaits me back home, particularly where my grandfather's concerned. I'd be lying if I said I was confident that he's going to change."

"Have you spoken to him?"

She sighed despondently and looked back at the view in front of them. City lights as bright as the observation deck with the display of fairy lights brightening the space. The sparkle of those lights twinkled in her eyes even while her tone was more somber.

"Machelle—you met her—she's been keeping an eye on him for me. But, no, he hasn't been picking up my calls. It's the same thing with my texts."

"I'm sorry." He grasped that she valued her relationship with her grandfather. Allowing his own broken ties with his family to color his impression of Lin's familial bond was erroneous. It also wouldn't bring him any closer to her. Not that he should want that. His concern now was purely based on the fact that they were work colleagues and friends.

He tucked aside his own confused emotions and focused on comforting her. "The distance could give you both space and time to think. *Absence makes the heart grow fonder* does actually apply sometimes."

Just not where my parents are concerned.

He couldn't say the same for her grandfather.

Lin tucked some of her faux locks behind her ear. The perfect blood-red strands matched the bold, red-tinged blush to the apples of her cheekbones and the eyeshadow framed by black mascara and the longest, most alluring lashes he'd ever seen. But then again, everything about her seemed to grab him more than anyone he knew.

She had left her coat back in the restaurant as he'd done. In her off-shoulder silky emerald wrap dress, she looked like a temptress who had been specially sent to drive him insane. It wasn't her fault she was so beautiful. Or that he was having this crazed reaction to her since he'd first laid eyes on her. This wasn't her problem, but entirely something that he had to own up to—*and put to bed*, he thought, and a fraction later he considered that maybe that wasn't the best choice of words.

The deck was rotating more slowly now, the evening winding down to a quicker close than he'd have liked.

Soon he was escorting her back upstairs, her hand resting like a branding iron on his arm.

Helping her into her coat, he slowed his hands to savor the feel of her under the thin peacoat she'd thought would protect her from the cold. At least her hands would be shielded from the winter elements in the hand warmer he'd given her.

She turned when he was done, her face tilted up to him, her lips a softer caramel red. Her mouth parted, and her eyes flickered over him, searching for something—he didn't know what.

Not until she said, "Can I kiss you?"

Karl's whole system went into shock. Very still for a long time, he finally regained the ability to move his head.

And he damned himself by nodding slowly and firmly.

Lin pulled up, watching him, and asher eyes closed, their lips touched.

The kiss was quiet but revelatory. His joy made up most of it, but her enthusiasm was the missing half. She kissed with her whole body, her hands gripping his arms and her soft chest pressing to his much harder one. He felt her breasts against him, her warmth through the coat that he'd have to keep her from wearing again, and almost naturally his arms circled around her waist and drew her closer to him.

They ended the kiss in a bittersweet way that reminded him of where they were and why they couldn't do it again.

Especially when Lin breathlessly apologized. "I'm sorry. I just had to be sure."

"Of?" he rasped back, just as winded from the lip-lock.

"I thought I was imagining our chemistry." She blinked up at him, long lashes fluttering temptingly. "I wasn't. Was I?"

"You weren't," he said.

"But we can't. I-I mean, we shouldn't be doing this."

"I know." Did it mean that he wanted to be reasonable? Not one bit. But she was right. They both had work to consider. And even if they were consenting adults, he knew that he couldn't offer her more than she might desire one day. It could be a kiss now; tomorrow, she could want love from him.

Karl should be relieved that she agreed they

should stop now that they'd proved the connection they had.

"Does this change anything?" she asked when he released her and she backed far enough away.

"No. Nothing's changed," he lied. The lie was worth it when she smiled shyly.

"Thanks for...not freaking out about...you know."

If he wasn't still a mess from their kiss, he might have joined in her nervous laughter. However, he *was* a mess, and he didn't think that anything would be the same for him again. Somehow a kiss had changed a lot more than he was comfortable with, and he didn't know what to do about it.

CHAPTER NINE

CHRISTMAS SNUCK UP on him.

One moment they were shoveling the first heavy snowfall right after Thanksgiving, then he was kissing Lin atop the Calgary Tower, and then December swung in with brutal weather and an equally taxing work schedule.

"Four Christmas parties should be our limit." Miranda kicked up her feet on his desk, either ignoring or unaware of the frown he swung her direction. "Seriously, I'm exhausted just watching you all work."

Nadine smiled benevolently. "Be thankful you weren't born to a large family. I'm flying out to my parents' this year, and I'm not looking forward to the possible flight delays."

Karl could foresee it. They'd been having inclement weather even for the hardy West.

"I have a couple big family gatherings. Also, I'm meeting Darius's parents and sisters and I told him I'm cool with it, but I'm low-key stressing at the same time." Miranda grinned nervously. It was unlike her to be anxious about anything. But she'd been dating her boyfriend for a year now, and not only did she seem to like him but it also sounded like the relationship was serious. Otherwise she wouldn't be meeting his family.

Karl thought of Isaiah. He'd kept his ex-boyfriend from meeting his parents. He had known that sweet and artsy Isaiah wouldn't ever be able to hold his own against Serenity and Charles Sinclair. His parents would have burned him with their icy attitudes. No matter how much Isaiah had asked to meet them, Karl had resolutely refused. Admittedly, he'd also been ashamed of his family after having met Isaiah's.

Of course, I shouldn't have to worry about that now.

Though, he had been doing his own low-key stressing. For the first time in years, he'd have his parents in the same room as him. He'd also be raising the stakes by confronting them in full view of his staff.

He'd have to be careful what he said in public around them. Controlling his emotions was imperative. He wouldn't let his parents get under his skin. Never again. Certainly not when he'd come so far without them supporting him.

Lin would get to meet them too.

His stomach did an extra, nauseating swoop at that fact, particularly as it was followed by the crystalline memory of having her in his arms, their lips touching and sliding against each other, his hands stroking her back and backside. She was a perfect fit in his arms. He'd loved holding her. Loved kissing her.

But he couldn't *love* her.

He couldn't love anyone. He'd been burned once by his parents, and then again by Isaiah. Moreover, Carrie was relying on him to come through for her during her special day with Stefon. He couldn't let either of them down by losing his focus now or distracting Lin from her work.

He'd just box away his feelings for her and hope that they died quietly, unacknowledged and unfulfilled.

"Just be yourself," he advised Miranda. It was all that he could tell her, as inexperienced as he was.

Nadine and Miranda eventually finished updating him. At the end, they had discussed the upcoming office Christmas party. It didn't matter that he'd avoided attending for so long. In the past, he'd flit in, make his rounds greeting everyone and then leave as quietly as he'd entered. He loved creating parties for other people; he didn't so much enjoy participating in them.

But with Christmas Eve right around the corner, they had some planning to do, and like always, Nadine and Miranda were in charge. He just signed off on whatever they suggested, fully trusting in their ability to do their best for the staff.

Karl had delved into his work after the two women left him.

He didn't glance up, not even when a knock sounded at his closed office door. "Come in."

"Am I interrupting you?" Lin's sweet, sexy voice drifted from the doorway. She had one foot in and one still out in the hallway, looking as though she wasn't sure whether to fully enter. Shyness overtaking her, she softly said, "I was hoping you could have lunch with me. I packed extra." She had a lunch bag in her hands, and it did look big enough to feed them both.

Karl's heart did what it was wont to do ever since they had kissed. It pumped faster and harder.

"Yeah. Lunch is good."

Her smile was brilliant, and she slipped into his office now more comfortably. He was curious as to how she did it. As he helped her clear his desk for their meal, he sneaked furtive glances at her. Was she not affected at all by what had happened between them? Because he'd been dreaming about it, and during the day, he found his mind meandering to that special moment. And it *had been* special. He could fight falling in love with her. What he couldn't deny was he'd liked kissing her and wanted desperately to do it again.

But she'd drawn a line there, and he would respect it.

"Are you working on the office party too?" Lin hovered closer to him, considering his dual monitors. He had the files open for Nadine's sketches on the party layout. They were hosting it in a trendy nightclub. The whole space would be cleared out for their staff party. "Miranda and Nadine have been talking about it nonstop."

"I'm not surprised," he mumbled.

She heard his tone and snapped her head to him. "Are you not going?"

"I'll show up. I always do. But I don't stay."

"Why not?" She handed him one of the club sandwiches she'd made. He smelled the smoked turkey and grilled cheese and stifled a ravenous groan.

Realizing they needed coffee, he held off from answering her to grab some cups, and when he was seated again, he finally said, "I'm not a partying kind of person."

She snorted. "You plan parties for a living."

"Ironic, I know," he said dryly. "You should look forward to it, though. The club's a hot spot in the city right now. Gives you a chance to check out the nightlife the city has to offer, even if most of the guests will be people you've met around the office." Everyone could bring a plus-one. Miranda was bringing her boyfriend, Darius. Nadine said she was dragging an old school friend along. He hadn't considered it because he wouldn't be hanging around the party for longer than was necessary for the boss to show his face.

"I've seen a few clubs already. It's not much different from what's available in Nairobi."

"Still, an opportunity to soak in Calgary while you have time."

She hummed in agreement around a mouthful of her sandwich.

"Of course, it's nice that you get to bring a plus-one." As he said it, he felt his heart rebel against him and jerk in protest. He clenched his jaws at the heavy oppression of jealousy squatting on his chest. The envy was, unfortunately, another side effect of kissing her. The thought of another person touching Lin, holding her and kissing her made him want to punch a wall in retaliation. Not that he'd ever behave inappropriately around her. She could bring anyone she wanted, and he wouldn't say or do a damn thing to stop her.

She's not mine to control.

She didn't belong to him, full stop.

He just had to get it through his thick skull.

"Any plans for Christmas besides the office party?" Lin asked when she finished her lunch. She sipped at her cooling coffee and watched him over the rim of her cup.

"Dinner at Carrie's." It was a standing tradition. Every Christmas Eve, Karl spent the evening with Carrie, Stefon and their grown kids and grandkids. Although he didn't like parties, he had to admit that he looked forward to the family gathering. It replaced the thought of what he hadn't had in his parents' cold home.

"Sounds familiar," she said with a warm smile.

"Actually, she's invited you again." Karl had nearly forgotten about it. "You should come." He tried for nonchalance, but his chest tightened in anticipation.

"I shouldn't intrude..." It had been what she'd said the first time.

"I'd love the company," he urged, voice hoarse with a rising need. It burgeoned out of nowhere and drilled him below the belt.

She shrugged lightly but smilingly. "All right." She turned away then to clean his desk of her lunch.

Karl freed a low, shaky breath, realizing the degree to which he'd been invested in her response. And now that he knew she was coming, he privately indulged in a smile of his own.

"Call me over the holidays," shouted Miranda across the parking lot. She waved and blew kisses enthusiastically while her good-natured, less drunk boyfriend escorted her gently into the back of a cab. Lin and Nadine waved back until they were gone.

Turning to her, Nadine said, "I should go too. I have a red-eye to catch, and I still have to wrap presents and pack and—" She broke off with a moan and then winked at something...or someone behind Lin.

"Have a good Christmas," Karl's deep, rumbling and sexy voice washed over her.

Half turning, she saw that he'd come up behind her and was far closer than she thought. And his eyes were on her. She tamped down the urge to shiver from the onslaught of pleasure in response to him.

"Merry Christmas to you both." Nadine walked away to her car.

"Truck's warmed and ready to go. Are you?" He had been busy heating the truck for her, insisting that she remain inside the club. She was glad he had. It was freezing outside. Temperatures had dropped drastically as the sun descended through the sky. But their night was far from over. They had a dinner at Carrie's ahead of them, and it had made sense for her to hitch a ride with Karl.

It also meant that he hadn't been able to leave the office party like he'd told her he usually did.

Not that he'd appeared to mind. He'd said that he didn't like parties, but he had been singing with her on a karaoke duet and cutting up the dance floor when Miranda and Nadine had asked the DJ to play some late-nineties R & B hits. What he hadn't done was drink a drop of alcohol. He was driving them to Carrie's, and he was taking his job seriously.

"Did you have fun?" she asked.

"It was…entertaining."

She laughed. "In other words, you had *fun*."

He chuckled at that, surprising her by the warmth and breadth of his grin.

Lin liked the silence that dispersed through the cabin. It was peaceful. She spent it admiring the holiday lights strung up all over the city. On the black branches of trees, on shop fronts and on the balconies of residential buildings. She cracked open the window and breathed in the refreshing wintry air. Now that she wasn't standing out in the cold, she liked how it brushed over her flushed face.

"Do you mind if I make a detour to my place?"

She looked back at him over her shoulder and shook her head. "Detour away." She was curious to see his place, and she tried to pretend she wasn't getting giddy as she peeled her eyes for the first sight of his home. Soon they had left behind the clustered buildings of downtown, and Karl was driving them past big, beautiful homes in a wealthy suburb.

Some of the houses were clearly historic buildings, their architecture still regal.

Quietly, he turned into the drive of the only unlit home on this side of the road.

"You don't have any lights up," she said, leaning forward and peeking up at his home through the snow gathering on the windshield.

He unbuckled his seat belt and opened his door, glancing back at the last moment. "You can come in."

When she followed him into his home, the first thing she noticed was the hush. And how cold it was. Shuddering, she willed her teeth to stop chattering and failed. Karl gestured her to trail after him once they both shucked their boots. He guided her to his family room. She should have known that it would be magnificent. She'd gotten a glimpse of the foyer when she'd entered and marveled at the vaulted ceiling with its impressive skylight and curved staircase with glossy wooden handrail and balustrades.

The family room was a mix of contemporary and traditional decor, with half the room covered in dark wood bookshelves, a home bar installed opposite the shelves, a pair of bold blue club chairs positioned in front of a gas fireplace. The earthy red brick of the fireplace surround and the emptiness of its wooden mantel was jarring. She'd have thought it a good place to put framed photos of his family.

He ushered her to the sofa and flicked on the dark fireplace.

In an instant the warmth of the hearth flickered to life and poured through her. Her jaws loosened and her whole body floated in bliss. She soon yawned and blinked blearily when the heat closed around her.

She hadn't been aware Karl had left her until he was with her again and holding out a mug.

Lin tasted it without asking and moaned when she recognized it was hot chocolate.

"I'll just be a second," he said before vanishing again.

He was gone for a while, but when he was back, her fatigue ripped away and she sat up alert. He had a cream-colored thin rectangular box in his hands. The box was elegantly wrapped with gold ribbon. It was definitely a present by the way he held it gently. But for whom, she didn't know.

She'd have sworn he was blushing, but he schooled his features into calm by the time he was close enough to the light of the fire to tell.

Karl sat by her with the box held out halfway.

"I know you don't celebrate Christmas, but I wanted to give this to you…"

"It's for me?" Heat spooled through her. Now she was blushing. "I didn't get anything for you." At his encouragement, she took the box and unwrapped it carefully. She gasped softly when she saw what lay inside.

She lifted the gold chain with its African pendant charm and fought the tears stabbing tiny knives into her eyes. "This is so sweet."

"I thought of you when I saw it." He evaded her eyes and nervously traced his mustache. She knew he was blushing now, and she was leaning in to give him more of a reason to be embarrassed. Before she reconsidered it, she kissed his cheek quickly and drew back, hearing his sharp inhale.

"What was that for?" he asked raspingly.

"I just wasn't expecting a gift." Not from him. He'd been incredibly generous to her, and he hadn't freaked out when she had kissed him that one time. Lin hadn't cast her mind there since it had happened. She'd initiated the kiss, sure. But she hadn't really thought he desired her back. Then he'd clutched her and returned her kiss with equal hunger and admitted that he felt the chemistry she had been feeling between them the whole time.

He brushed the spot she'd kissed on his cheek and lowered his hand, frowning.

Lin's chest rose and fell faster as he stared at her.

His eyes dropped to her mouth. She licked her lips.

Slowly, he pulled into her, giving her plenty of time to push him back by the time his breath mingled with hers. She should have stopped them. The risk of endangering their unlikely but growing friendship was a very real thing that scared her. She was already facing the possibility of never having the same relationship with her grandfather again. He hadn't spoken to her since she'd left. She didn't want the same happening with Karl.

Was losing Karl worth another of his forbidden kisses?

Yes, she decided. And without another thought, she pressed her lips to his like she had before.

He recovered much quicker this time. Lifting her up, he settled her in his lap, her legs wrapping around him instinctually. Karl scorched her mouth with his fiery kisses, his lips expertly stroking hers, his tongue coaxing hers to play, and his hands smoothing over her back and drawing her nearer to his loving.

"Stay with me," he panted, his eyes unfocused, glazed with his longing—an echo of everything she was feeling right then.

She cupped his strong jaw and kissed him slow and long.

It was all the answer he needed.

Lifting her up with him and chuckling low and huskily when she yelped in his ear, he carried her upstairs, and a moment later she was sprawled atop his massive, comfortable bed with him on top of her and their dinner plans forgotten to their passion.

CHAPTER TEN

LIN DIDN'T KNOW how her mom had done it.

All those years ago when she had packed up and called it quits, leaving her daughter and husband behind. She'd eventually sent along the request for a divorce, and Lin knew from her grandfather that she had since remarried and had other children. She still couldn't grasp how easy it had seemed in her mind for her mother to walk away. It had been a selfish thing to do… but maybe it had made her happier.

And maybe it had been selfish of Lin to sleep with Karl. She could certainly say she'd been happy in the moment. She was still floating on cloud nine from the bliss of being with him.

Beside her, he stirred, his eyes cracking open, and his smile indicating he felt as replete as she did.

"Rise and shine," she teased, looking up to where a shaft of moonlight spilled through his half-turned bedroom blinds. "Well, then again, maybe not."

She stroked along his chest, fingers skimming between his flexing pecs, his abs clenched in response to her touch, and his breath quickened. He caught her by the wrist right as she reached the waistband of his black boxer shorts. She didn't remember him pulling them on. But she'd been so boneless by the time he'd been done with her that she wasn't shocked her memory had some holes in it. All she knew perfectly well was that he'd satisfied her thoroughly. And judging by the way he gazed at her adoringly, kissed her tender inner wrist and stroked his thumb where his lips touched her, he had been no less affected by her.

"Too soon," he murmured at her.

There they'd have to disagree. She descended, and he met her kiss halfway. She draped herself over him and gasped into their tangled mouths when he flipped her over with a rumbling growl.

He reached between them, and a second later the hot, heavy and very thick evidence of his desire yielded against her naked quivering flesh.

She arched her back with an eagerness to unite them again.

His phone rang from somewhere across the room. They both groaned at the interruption.

"Ignore it," she moaned and locked her heels behind his back.

Karl seemed happy to oblige, but then it rang again. And again. And finally she loosened her legs and moaned, "On second thought, answer it and then put it on silent."

He laughed gruffly; the sound as pleasant as the sex had been. "It's my godmother," he reported and returned to bed.

She sat up at that. "Oh, no! Carrie's dinner."

Karl gripped her hand and pulled her back onto the bed before she scampered away from him. He wrapped his arms and caged her to him.

Lin gently pushed at his chest. "We're going to be late," she rushed breathlessly, more from the fact that his face was close to hers, and she could feel his rigid erection under her.

"No, we're not. Dinner is over by now, and I already let Carrie know that we would be... indisposed."

She stared at him with a new mortification. "You didn't tell her..." She couldn't complete the sentence, her face on fire from the thought of it alone.

His laughter frothed up around her and matched the way he cuddled her closer.

"Give me more credit than that. If Carrie knew you were here with me right now, she'd switch her event to my wedding." He stiffened suddenly, his muscles tauter, and his voice more strained when he added hastily, "Not that anyone's getting married."

"Of course not," she murmured.

She didn't know what else to say. He knew his godmother better. But it sounded about right. If she'd told her grandfather that she and Karl had… She blushed more furiously.

Let's just say that it's not something I want happening. Ever.

"It's late. Do you want to stay?"

She had her head resting on his shoulder and her naked body curled up to the warmth of him. There was enough natural lighting to see, but even without it she could hear the longing threaded in his voice and the heat spilling through his shadowed eyes.

Not for the first time, she questioned whether she was being selfish like her mother had been. She wanted to stay with him, but she knew realistically that this—whatever this forbidden fling was—would not last. She had a home in Kenya; he had one right here in Calgary. She worked with him, and she would be relying on his strong networking connections once she opened the doors of her own company.

She'd tossed aside her usual selflessness once already when she'd left her grandfather to pursue her dream. She would be gambling her newfound friendship with Karl for another incomparably perfect moment with him.

He dropped a kiss on her forehead, and she angled her head back, knowing exactly what she was going to do.

"I'll stay," she whispered and closed her eyes as he kissed her again.

Two nights.

He'd had Lin in his arms and his bed for two whole nights before they had to resurface out of his home on the day after Christmas. It hadn't been how he planned to spend his holidays, but they had been the best few days, that he'd had in a long while.

It was why his heart sank a little on the morning that she was leaving.

"I can't believe it's the first day of Kwanzaa already," she chirped beside him at his breakfast table. She was cheery for the early morning. Something he'd gotten used to in a short amount of time.

To think that he would have to recall what it had been like without her.

His thinking grew gloomier as the morning whizzed by and it came time for her to leave. She had suffered without her wardrobe and toiletries for two days, just to make him happy. But now she needed to drop by her apartment before they had to go back to work. He hadn't forgotten that the first day of Kwanzaa was also the beginning of Carrie's weeklong events leading up to her vow renewal.

Right before they walked out the front door, he looked around his home, at the lights and tinsel she'd looped around his staircase banister and the Christmas tree she'd had him rummage out of his storage in the basement so they could decorate together, and he sniffed the air that faintly smelled of their copious baking last night. Sugar cookies and a Kenyan fried-dough dish she had called *mandazi*. They'd been more delicious than the sugar cookies.

The lump in his throat had nothing to do with him missing her already.

"It's so sparkly." Lin looked back at him with her hand tossed up to shield her eyes from the bright white snow, but her lovely eyes squinched, anyways.

Okay, maybe he was moping a bit more than he thought he would.

Just like he knew he'd miss her more than he ever believed possible.

Checking another item off the list, Karl trekked from the food truck supplying their dinner for the evening to the big white tent on the white lawn. Snow tumbled lightly from the gray skies.

He had to take bigger steps to keep from tripping and falling face first.

Inside, the tent was bustling. The earliest guests had arrived and more were trickling in in a steady stream. Miranda was positioned at the entrance to the tent, clipboard in hand, matching names and guiding Carrie and Stefon's guests to their seats on the seating chart. Nadine was going around checking on the heaters once again, moving them so that the tent was evenly heated and none of the guests were aware of the decline in temperature outdoors. The head table was empty for now, but his godmother would be making her grand entrance later on, once everyone else had arrived.

The tent flaps opened, and in walked Lin.

His heart stuttered.

She saw him immediately and veered in his direction. He took in her hair, her bright red faux locks bundled high on the middle of her head. She wore a colorfully geometric dress that made her rosy-brown skin lovelier, and the strappy black heels winding up her smooth calves had his mind slipping into gutter territory. She looked like an African goddess. The best part was the familiar gold necklace sitting right above the soft swell of her cleavage.

"It looks amazing," she said as soon as she was within earshot of him. She clutched the African charm pendant and looked around with that innocent expression of awe he'd grown used to. He knew that she was used to luxury and it wasn't the splendor of his events that threw her, rather the sentimental touches that were specific to Carrie's Kwanzaa-themed romantic event. "This place was empty when you sent me photos this morning."

He'd come here right after dropping Lin off at her apartment to shower and change. She had lived with him for two days without complaint that she was missing her home. He figured she'd been happy to get a little privacy back. Inexplicable bitterness flavored his tongue as he looked away and tried to see the tent through her eyes.

The decor was African in style. Rustically elegant wood-framed low sofas. Colorful print fabric interspersed with softer, muted shades of browns, beiges and greens. Found objects like feathers, horns and vividly bright African flora were gathered together in handcrafted wooden jars at each table. The plate settings were copper chargers and rich and earth-toned reds, oranges and greens for the tablecloths and napkins. The place cards were simply the names of the guests in elegant calligraphy in Lin's own hand. She'd done them for the event without asking, but he liked how they'd turned out.

The head table was even more special.

A sparkling swath of fabrics in red, green and black swept down in arches and was pinned above a chandelier that dangled in the middle. The lighting fixture floated right above the special *kinara* that Lin had designed and printed for Carrie and Stefon. He peeked at Lin and noted that she saw it, her wide, joy-filled smile giving her away. Similar decor and color theme adorned the long table along with two gold thronelike chairs for the happy couple renewing their vows. It was coming together nicely... and hopefully quickly, as he blinked and noticed the tent was filling up.

"You should grab your seat." He didn't want her getting caught waiting as a line was beginning to form between the tables.

Lin hesitated, just staring up at him for a moment, but then she squeezed his hand and turned away. It looked like she'd wanted to say something. Whatever it was, he would have to wait to ask her. He had a party to manage.

Carrie and Stefon made a touching speech thanking the guests who'd attended the first of their many scheduled events for the last week of the year. At the end, they lit the central black candle on the *kinara* and spoke the opening phrase to any Kwanzaa festivity: *"Habari gani?" How are you?* The greeting in Lin's native tongue was familiar and comforting. As was the returning chorus of *"Habari gani?"* from other guests.

Dinner came after, and Lin chatted easily with Nadine and Miranda on one side. The chair on her other side was empty, though. Karl had left again to monitor the caterers this time. He'd done it in lieu of Nadine because Lin knew he wanted everything to run smoothly for his god-mother.

"Don't look now, but I think that means trouble," Miranda leaned in to whisper, her eyes glued to the tent's entrance.

Lin lowered her fork and knife, the perfectly seasoned salmon and asparagus on her plate left to wait while she observed the newcomers. An older man and woman standing stiffly side by side but decked in head-to-toe designer clothing. The woman wore a gray fur stole and a figure-hugging sparkling dress the color of red wine. The man had gold cufflinks and a brilliant gold Rolex. Their brown skin shone like they'd spent hours in a spa, but their furrowed brows and pruned lips implied otherwise. They appeared wound-up about something, and they only got worse when Karl returned from minding the caterers and approached them.

"His parents," Miranda hissed right into her ear.

Lin startled. She'd been so absorbed by the family drama that she had forgotten she wasn't alone in spectating. She would've guessed they were his parents just by the way Karl had met them. Even from this distance, he looked like he was preparing for war.

"Are they not close?" Lin had wanted to ask him but missed her chance during Thanksgiving. Besides, she didn't think he would've answered her then. They hadn't been as close as they were now. A lot had transpired between them since...

Like having sex.

She blushed at that.

"We don't know." Nadine shrugged her one bare shoulder, her asymmetrical dress shimmering under the dazzling lighting overhead. "He doesn't discuss his family all that much. I know he has a lot of siblings. Three...or maybe it was four. Karl's always been pretty private about his personal life."

"But you're probably right, Lin. It doesn't look like a cozy family reunion, does it?" Miranda clicked her tongue and shook her head, but her glossy updo remained undisturbed. She must have had hundreds of bobby pins to hold all her hair up like that.

"Poor Karl," Nadine murmured in agreement.

"Yeah," Lin added forlornly.

She wasn't exactly in the best place with her grandfather either. It was hard watching Karl interact with his parents when it was obvious that there weren't any warm feelings between the two parties. She clamped her teeth into her bottom lip and realized she wouldn't be able to eat another bite until he was sitting next to her. Just as Lin envisioned herself standing and walking over to intervene, she saw Carrie and Stefon heading in the same direction, and she hoped it was to Karl's rescue.

Sure enough, Karl stepped away when his godmother patted his arm, and he stalked off—in the opposite direction of where Lin sat. He disappeared past a tent flap in the back of the tent where the caterers and waitstaff were coming in and out.

Lin's spirit deflated. She'd thought he would come over to her.

Why would he? Nothing's changed.

That wasn't true. Plenty had changed in a couple of days. She had gone beyond fantasizing about him to experiencing what it would be like waking up draped in his scent and wrapped by his body. She knew she was catching feelings, yet she couldn't stop herself from liking him. It wasn't an on-and-off switch she could easily flip when convenient to her. She shouldn't want to like him either. Shouldn't desire anything more. Not even another of his tasty kisses...

He also didn't seem interested in continuing how they'd spent the past two days.

It's for the best, Lin chided herself.

This way she could finish working without distractions. It just also happened to be the best way to protect her heart from the disappointment of a rejection.

CHAPTER ELEVEN

A CHORUS OF *"Habari gani?"* rose up from the workshop.

More and more of Carrie's guests were filtering into the space, and soon all the workstations were at full capacity. It was the day after the dinner in the tent, and they were enjoying the next event on the list that would culminate in Carrie and Stefon's vow-renewal ceremony. But there were still a few days until it was New Year's and the end of Kwanzaa.

Lin saw Karl. She paused, hesitating about whether to go to him.

Nadine and Miranda were already sharing a table with two other people. There wouldn't be room for her there.

But a cursory look around the room showed her that there were other tables with space for her. It would save her an awkward conversation with him. Since he'd disappeared from the tent yesterday, she'd only briefly glimpsed him when she had been on her way home. But Karl hadn't shown signs that he had seen her leaving. And she wasn't confident that she wouldn't be disturbing him had she gone up to say good-night.

Now here she was, deciding whether to avoid him again or not.

She wasn't any closer to a decision when Miranda hollered her name and caught the attention of everyone in the room. Heads turned toward her. Lin blushed, embarrassed at being in the spotlight. She waved shyly at Miranda and intended to walk over to greet her and Nadine, only her eyes locked onto Karl's.

He watched her, his mouth a long, even line, his face calm. None of the frustration he'd barely restrained around his parents yesterday marred his beautifully perfect face right now. Lin was staring at the man who had made sweetly explosive love to her.

She lowered her hand slowly and took a step toward Karl.

He nodded at her imperceptibly.

Lin smiled back, her doubt vanishing for now.

"Hey," she greeted him warmly, her face steadily growing hotter the longer the two other people at their station stared at her.

"Hey," he echoed. There was a small lift on one side of his mouth. A barely-there smile that was just for her.

She opened her mouth to ask him if everything was all right with his parents but stopped herself at the last second. He might not like her prying into his life. The last thing she wanted was to put a wedge between them. They had a short time left together, and even if she couldn't kiss him again, she didn't want to ruin whatever it was their relationship had become.

I'll miss him.

A sadness rolled through her at the thought. It had happened more often now as she crossed the final days off her mental calendar. Her plane ticket was booked for a week after New Year's Day. She had gone into this knowing she'd be leaving behind the friends and the happy memories she had created in Canada. Still, it was hard to psych herself up for it.

Harder now that she had someone she was going to miss a whole lot.

Casting Karl a sidelong glance, she felt another heart-wrenching pang.

The workshop starting was a good excuse for a distraction.

They were taking a pottery class. Carrie was good friends with the black business owners of the workshop. As part of her Kwanzaa event, she'd wanted as many of her guests as possible to experience African culture, modern and historical. Lin understood the owners were siblings, and they were leading the beginner-level workshop for the day.

A quick look around and she counted nearly two dozen eager workshop participants. It was a good turnout for a weekday evening. Lin had worried that a weeklong event might deter some of the guests, and it had some, just not as many as she'd thought. Clearly Carrie and Stefon had strong friendships in the city and the kind of support an upstanding couple like them deserved. Sadly, there was no sign of Karl's parents.

He'd looked so wound-up after the encounter with them. She commiserated with his plight and the difficulty of having hard-to-deal-with family. It couldn't be easy for him. To add to his problems, he was probably avoiding confrontation for Carrie's and Stefon's sakes.

Lin spotted his godmother.

Carrie saw her too and waved to them from one of the front tables. She nudged Stefon, and he raised a hand in greeting as well. Their enthusiasm was infectious. Lin only hoped it was a good omen for how the rest of the day would be. Or at least how the workshop would pan out.

Once the general introductions and explanations were made by the hosts and the workshop owners, she felt Karl's eyes on her. She looked up and confirmed he was staring at her.

That small smile briefly brushed his lips. "First time throwing on a wheel?"

"First time, period," she confessed, wincing. She loved trying new things, but she didn't want to outright embarrass herself in front of Karl. And throwing mud on a wheel could get messy. She knew that much.

Aprons and protective eyewear were passed around. Karl offered to help her tie the stays of her apron, and then he turned his back for reciprocation. As she tied a double knot, he said, "It's not hard. I'll help teach you."

Before she had a chance to question him, the workshop instructors called for their attention and began a demonstration of how to wedge the clay and prepare it for centering on the wheel head. She watched the same demonstration as everyone else, but when it came time to try her hand at pottery making for the first time, she couldn't recreate what she'd just seen demonstrated.

"It won't stay centered. Why won't it stay centered?" she grumbled under her breath.

She felt Karl's reassuring presence at her side, and she all too naturally leaned in to him, forgetting where they were until she heard Carrie's sparkling laughter from the other side of the room. Cheeks flushed hot, she gave him space and muttered, "Sorry." Little slips like that would land them in the kind of trouble she understood he wouldn't desire. Fielding questions from his staff and from Carrie weren't high on her priority list either. Not when it was general knowledge that she'd be leaving for home once she was done here.

"You're not applying even pressure from the top and side." He came up behind her then and sealed the personal space she'd just given him. With his hands on top of hers, he guided her palms and fingertips to coax cooperation from the red clay on her wheel. "More water. Your hands have to be wet, but not too wet."

He was all around her, his hard chest to her back, and his arms cocooning her closer to him. The scent of his cologne infiltrating her senses and making her brain chemically respond. The smoothness and bigness of his hands engulfing hers. Physically, she was turning to mush. Instead of feeling crowded by him, she wanted to snuggle into him more.

"Just like that. Not too hard, and none too gentle. You're the master. The clay will do what you want it to, but you can't force it either. Lean in, hold firm and gently steer it into doing what you want it to do."

"Got it," she croaked, biting her lip to stop from whimpering when his fingers caressed the back of her hands.

It was a more intimate demonstration than the one the workshop instructors had given.

When Karl moved away to his station, leaving her to practice what he'd taught her in his very hands-on demo, she couldn't help but wonder what might have happened had they been in the workshop alone, just the two of them.

She was having more fantasies of the same ilk.

It wasn't good that she was forming the attachment that she should be avoiding. She could have all the fun she wanted, but she didn't want to leave any piece of her behind with him. Worse for her if that piece turned out to be her heart.

The end of the workshop came too swiftly for her taste. She'd been enjoying herself a little too much. Not that her clay would tell you that. It was...not anything that she would want anyone to fire and glaze.

Case in point, Carrie walked over with a tray to collect Lin's piece for firing. Karl's godmother stopped by her wheel, and her mouth formed a little *O*.

"Is it a mug or a bowl?" she asked.

"I wish I knew." Lin snorted with laughter. Carrie laughed too, but she still insisted on glazing her masterpiece for her.

Carrie whistled when she paused behind her godson, finally bringing Lin's attention to Karl's wheel. She nearly whistled her appreciation as well. Stunned didn't begin to describe what she felt when she saw his finished piece.

He'd crafted a small teapot: stem, lid and all.

She wasn't alone in admiring what he had produced in the short allotted time of the workshop.

The other two guests at their workstation circled his space too, complimenting him.

Some other participants and guests of Carrie and Stefon gathered to praise the teapot—easily the best piece crafted there that evening.

"Show off," Carrie joked, taking his teapot for the baking and glazing that would be done in the back room.

"I should have known you were a pro at this when you were helping me," said Lin as soon as they were alone, the other guests drifting off to a break room in the back that had been converted to a small snacking area with refreshments and even music as entertainment. She shook her head laughingly. "But I'll admit you surprised me. Pottery as a talent."

"I can juggle too," he said with a lopsided smile.

She laughed harder, wiping at the tears pricking her eyes and gasped, "I don't even know who you are." Laughter slowing, she realized just how true that was, yet she still didn't find it a fault. If they had more time left, she would use it unwrapping the mysteries that shrouded him and peeling back the many layers to his heart.

Stopping herself before she started dwelling on it, she tipped her head to the exit.

"It'll take time before our art has baked. Did you want to go for a walk?"

It would give them time together. She only wished she had more of it to spend with him.

Calgary was beautiful at night. Somehow the winter nights right after a decent snowfall were the best. City lights glowing better off the white snow that hadn't browned yet. The air crisp with a chill that took your breath away. The city quieter under the blanket of fresh snow. Karl would almost say it was romantic if he believed in romance and love. Not wanting to ruin the moment with pointless thoughts, he concentrated on what he did have.

Right now it was this nascent but transient bond with Lin.

She was leaving: that was inevitable. He'd known it when he'd hired her services, and he understood it when they had agreed to start a physical relationship. Yet as that time inched closer and closer, he had begun to acknowledge it more with every day that passed—every day that was one day less with Lin.

"I'll need to seriously warm up after this with

a cup of tea." Beside him, Lin huddled into her coat, another thin peacoat that wasn't made to withstand the cold.

They had walked far enough from the pottery workshop for him to be all right with risking putting an arm over her shoulders and drawing her closer to the warmth he could provide. She sagged under his embrace, curling into his side, and wrapping her own arm around his waist for support.

Reflexively, he pressed a kiss to her temple, smiling when she hummed her pleasure.

That was how they entered the café he had in mind.

Once they had their orders, they grabbed a table with a view of the street and the snow that had piled there over the day in massive drifts. He was partly glad it wasn't snowing anymore. It would make driving Lin to his home safer. *See? Even that.* Before her, he hadn't had thoughts like that. Somehow her safety was paramount now, and he was too tired to argue or silence the instinct.

"So...pottery. What's up with that?" she asked, her cup of black tea warming her hands, her eyes brighter and her skin looking less chaffed by the cold weather they'd walked through for their prize of caffeine.

"When I was in school, I took a course, and

then I did a few months of apprenticeship with a local ceramist." He had thought he'd forgotten the skills of the trade, but the workshop today was a reminder that he still possessed a talent for and interest in it.

"You wanted to work with ceramics," she said, sounding less shocked and more engaged in his past dream.

"It was a long time ago, but yes. It was a career path I'd seriously considered."

She seemed to have forgotten her tea, and he couldn't help but notice she was a little too engaged for his comfort. Especially when she asked, "What happened to change your mind? How did you go from training ceramist to event planner extraordinaire?"

Karl gazed into his cup and felt the scowl tipping his mouth down. He should have seen this coming. Should have known that he wasn't ready to talk about it, let alone to relive the memories tied to his old career dream.

But Lin was waiting on his reply, and he'd dug this hole, so he had to see it through wherever it led him. "My parents didn't approve." It was a simple answer. The plain, ugly truth too. His parents hadn't wanted a son of theirs doing anything that wouldn't directly benefit the family businesses. They'd berated him until it was too much to bear and he had caved in to their wish to see him doing something else with his life. Something *they* approved of.

Of course, that hadn't turned out the way they wanted either.

"They didn't like my ceramics, so I quit." It had just been one more thing that his parents had controlled in his life. "I was lucky that I found something else I enjoy equally and I'm good at. It just wasn't working on a potter's wheel with muddy fingers."

He didn't have to give Lin the playback or go into in-depth explanation. She had a sympathetic look ready for him.

"They were trying to control you," she surmised sadly, and he realized that this hit home for her too. She had done all of this—paused her life in Kenya and worked with him because she wanted to prove her ability to her grandfather. He knew family could be toxic. He knew they could be good but still find ways to hurt you.

His parents hadn't done him any good. Except maybe instill in him the drive to be his own boss.

"They still try. If I let them, they'd be happy."

"Your answer was to stop everything." Her bottom lip actually trembled.

Karl balled his hand into a fist so he wouldn't lose the battle to reach out and comfort her. It was one thing for him to loathe reliving his past but another to see her torn up about it on his behalf. He didn't like to see her upset. "I was young, impressionable. At the time I really believed them when they said that I'd be fine without it. I didn't realize that they were trying to change me to suit their tastes." They'd played the same game with his siblings. Cyrus had been the only one who had jumped at their command. They had done everything possible to suppress their individuality. In the end, all they'd accomplished was pushing their children away.

"You shouldn't have stopped. You shouldn't let them win now. You're so good at pottery."

He snorted humorlessly, one dry note that was half bark, half laugh. "That may be so, Lin, but I'm not quitting what I do or closing my company."

"I didn't say that you should. As a hobby, maybe?"

He hadn't thought of that before. After his parents had crushed his dream, he'd packed it away with the intent never to revisit it. Lin hadn't known that he used to do ceramics, so she couldn't have known that it would dredge up this old grudge he had against his parents. Maybe it was the universe's way of giving him another chance.

A chance he wouldn't have considered if he hadn't had this talk with Lin.

"A hobby perhaps," he agreed.

She rewarded him with a smile. A smile that he wanted pressed to his mouth. Before he talked himself out of it, he leaned over the table separating them, and he touched his lips to hers. He melted when she sighed into their connected mouths, her mewl coiling around his pounding heart like her hands clinging to his shoulders and pulling him closer.

This, he thought, *is why it'll be hard to let her go.*

In that instant, he knew he would trade all the ceramic talent he had for an extra day or two with her. He just didn't know what to do about it.

CHAPTER TWELVE

THE NEXT FEW days blended together for Karl. It was as though he had taken the longest blink of his life, and he'd jumped three, four days into the future, and now it was all that much closer to counting down to the New Year and the end of Kwanzaa.

It also meant Carrie's vow renewal with her husband was fast approaching.

And that means Lin's leaving soon.

He didn't want to worry about that now, though. He had plenty of time to do it *after* Carrie's celebration. The festive mood was in full swing today as Carrie, Stefon, her family and guests were skating. Not everyone was wearing skates, however. A few guests had braved trying the ice bikes that the city park had made available to borrow. Miranda whizzed by on one of them, narrowly missing him. Nadine was hot on her trail. Apparently, they were racing around the perimeter of the wide pond. Karl shook his head, smiling, but he lost that smile when he looked around the people sharing the patch of blue ice with him on that frosty winter afternoon, and he saw that Lin wasn't among them.

She was still nowhere to be seen.

He'd dropped her off at her place to change out of last night's outfit. They had been to another event yesterday and gone back to his home together. If she showed up wearing the same outfit, someone would suspect something. He had wanted to pick her up, but she'd insisted that she could find her way to the park, reminding him that he'd brought her here before when they had been enjoying the leaves together there. It was hard to think that had only been a couple of months ago.

He had always been attracted to her. From the moment he had set eyes on her, there had been this chemical pull she had on him. Then he had learned she felt the same, and they'd embarked on an affair.

An affair that was ending soon.

He didn't need the reminder. What he needed was for Lin to get here so he could stop worrying and wondering whether he should go and fetch her himself. But he understood that space was healthy. They'd spent so much time together in the last week she needed her own time to do her own things. All healthy relationships shared this foundation—

But he wasn't in a relationship with her, not in that sense of the word.

They were lovers. This thing between them was purely physical, sexual.

Romance and love had never been part of the equation. He wasn't sending her flowers, or lighting candles aside from the ones they had for Kwanzaa every night. He sure as heck wasn't falling for her…

Had he fallen for her?

It would explain this nostalgia he'd been struggling with every time he thought of her and replayed their time spent together. He had felt something like this with Isaiah. That was when he'd lost his head and heart to his boyfriend. When he had loved him. Karl froze on the ice rink. He'd been gliding slowly on his skates the whole while, the pace reflecting his deep thinking. Moving aside out of respect for the other skaters, he stood on the bank, hands on his hips, and his face turned up to the gray clouds blotting the blue sky.

He knew he'd felt this way before. Done this dance before. Sung this same song.

No, it's different with Lin than it was with Isaiah.

With Isaiah it had been a roller-coaster. All

wild, hot, with flimsy restraints and no quick way to stop. The crash-and-burn of his heartbreak should have been expected. Isaiah hadn't wanted to be saddled with the mess he'd become after his parents had kicked him out. In all fairness, he had been confused and angry and hurt.

With Lin it hadn't been a four-alarm fire. Their time together was less volatile but still so passionate she'd left an indelible impression on him. So not the exact same shade or flavor that he'd once had with Isaiah but adjacent. More addicting, that was for certain. Part nostalgia, the other part was just frighteningly new.

But I loved Isaiah...

Following that logic, he loved Lin. Had fallen in love with her sometime in the span of meeting her and carrying her to his bed.

Karl had scratched the surface of his realization when he heard Lin's name.

Miranda and Nadine were calling out to her from the pond's icy surface.

Breathlessly, he sought her out with his eyes and then breathed easier when he saw it was her. She looked perfectly fine too, which eased his concern that she had somehow been delayed by disaster, and then he saw who was walking with her.

The blood in his veins chilled and congealed. But the iciness that gripped him didn't root his skates to the frozen lake. He skated forward, gliding choppily in his haste to reach where Lin was with his brother, Cyrus. Behind them, his parents looking as foreboding as they always had.

As they always will.

The only thing keeping him from charging faster to them was that Lin looked comfortable. She was gesturing with her hands and smiling, and Cyrus looked down at her like a big grinning fool.

Karl ground his teeth when his older brother threw back his head and laughed loudly and obnoxiously. God. It was the same annoying sound he'd had to deal with when they'd been children and Cyrus had gotten the upper hand by having their parents take his side in their squabbles. That laughter had haunted him once. Now it just grated badly.

But his blood boiled when Cyrus touched Lin's shoulder and beamed that stupid grin of his down at her.

Enough.

With an angry boost in energy, he leaped onto the embankment and stopped before them.

His parents, Cyrus and Lin all came to a halt, eyes widening at the sight of him.

"Karl," his mom said and smiled, but it rang as forced and tight.

His dad just grumbled under his breath. He didn't catch any of it, but he knew it wasn't anything that could be said in decent company.

Ignoring them, he drilled his focus on Lin. "What took you so long?"

Her eyes doubled in size, and she darted a look from him to his parents before saying softly, "I lost the key to my luggage, so I couldn't grab my favorite jeans." Then, after a beat of silence, she added, "I hope you weren't worried."

He realized he was acting a fool over a wardrobe mishap. It would have been embarrassing if it had been the two of them, but he'd done it in front of his family. Clenching his teeth, he avoided the press of their stares—and in Cyrus's case, that smarmy grin of his—just knowing that if he looked their way, he would feel worse than he already did.

Lin was frowning lightly, her eyes reflecting the same unease he'd experienced when she had been away from him.

"I wanted to go over a few of your latest designs and prints." He was lying through his teeth. He trusted whatever she had produced for Carrie's events so far. She hadn't disappointed him, not once, and he didn't see the point in looking over her shoulder. Not when she'd started, and not now. But he had to say something to backtrack this humiliation.

"Right now?" she asked.

He jerked his head affirmatively and whirled back to the ice, knowing that she would follow.

Lin stared at the top of Karl's bald head. He had guided her to a bench near the skate-rental place. He had come back with a pair, and it wasn't until he started lacing her up that she realized that she hadn't, in fact, told him her size. Still, he had somehow gotten it right. She had no complaints about pinched toes or poor blood circulation in her feet. Standing with a little wobble, she smiled gratefully when he grasped her hands and helped her onto the ice.

She hadn't forgotten how she'd ended up skating with him.

"What's this about my latest prints?"

"Nothing. They're perfect," he said.

She squeezed his hands and struggled to concentrate on where her feet were on the ice. She wanted to look into his eyes when she asked this next part.

"Were you luring me away from your parents and brother?"

"I hadn't expected they'd show up." A valid answer, yet she heard something in his voice that had her suspecting there was more he wasn't saying.

She let his answer be what it was for a while,

focusing on his hands holding hers, his skates expertly sliding backward despite every jerk forward by her. Once they'd done a full circuit of the ice and avoided any mishaps along the way, she trailed back to what they had been discussing. His family's unexpected arrival and his tense reaction to them.

"Aren't you going to ask why I showed up with them?" she asked.

Karl helped her transition off the ice back onto less slippery ground. He stayed standing when she dropped onto a bench and peered up at him.

"I figured there was a good reason." That might be so, but his closed-off expression suggested otherwise.

"We bumped into each other in the parking lot. They asked for directions, and I told them I was part of Carrie's party too."

"See," he said gruffly, looking more satisfied than he had a second earlier, "a perfectly sound reason."

Lin desperately wished she could let him off with that comment, but she needed to know if having his family so near was hurting him.

Why? Because I think he wants comfort.

She knew Karl presented himself as this strong, emotionally resistant person, but she also understood it had to be tough on him, dealing with whatever bad blood existed between him and his parents and brother, and keeping his head on straight to make Carrie and Stefon's celebratory events as amazing as they were as individuals and a couple.

That was why she had to talk to him.

Patting the space on the bench beside her, she said, "I think there's more to what you're not saying. I don't want you holding it in."

"I don't know what you mean."

"Pushing it down and pretending it doesn't exist might make you feel better now, but it doesn't make the problem go away."

He jutted his jaw out and clenched it. "There isn't a problem."

"If that were true, you'd have been able to look them in the eyes. Instead, you ignored them and walked off with me." She threw up her hands. "I don't know what you'd call that, but I'd say it was a problem."

She watched his shoulders draw back and his thick black brows slam down. That dense wall of defense was sliding into place.

"They're Carrie's guests. Not mine."

Lin was losing him. Any second now he'd tell her off and walk away. She didn't want that happening. Not when all she wanted was to help ease the burden he was shouldering. A burden that had to do with his family and whatever had driven him to be at odds with them.

"Okay. I know when to back off."

Karl's frown didn't look as scary as it had a second earlier. "It's not your fault." He locked his hands between his legs and looked out at the frozen pond. His scowl stormed over his face when she saw his line of sight aligned with his parents and brother. She knew who he was blaming, but she didn't understand how it had gotten to be this bad.

"Why are you angry with them?" she coaxed softly, in hopes that he would open up to her.

"They kicked me out."

It was said bluntly, so that she didn't miss any of the bitterness roughening his voice.

"Why?" she choked after the shock passed.

"Simple. My parents decided I wasn't ever going to fit that perfect mold they had in their minds of what their children should be like."

She reached for him instinctively, her hand on his leg offering a comforting squeeze.

He didn't seem to register her touch, his gaze focused on the distance and his voice growing harder and angrier. "It was the same with my other siblings too. All except Cyrus." He sneered his brother's name, and she didn't recognize him at that moment. The mask fully stripped, the pain and rage fighting for a place to control him. "Cyrus was their golden boy. He tattled on us. Bullied us. All because he didn't want to *be* us. He had their favor, and he wanted it more than he wanted a relationship with his brothers and sister."

"What about your other siblings?" Surely they'd have bonded over Cyrus's ill treatment of them.

But she guessed she was wrong when Karl pried his jaws apart to grit out, "You'd think we would be closer, but no. Our parents pushed us to compete our whole lives. It was always about one-upping each other. Cyrus did it best, but we all played the game when we were younger, when it was easier to believe that we were fighting for our parents' attention and love instead. It took a long while to realize they didn't have any love to give us. They never had."

"Karl…" She didn't know what else to say to him.

"We never fully healed from that trauma. I can't remember the last time I spoke to or saw my brothers and sister."

"And your parents? How long has it been since…" She couldn't bring herself to say it again, her heart breaking for him.

"Long enough to know that they'd done the best thing for me when they pushed me away." He pushed to his feet and swung that gloomy scowl on her. "I'm better without them in every regard. I just need them to see that I never needed them."

She was on her shaky feet as well, the skates not deterring her from pressing a hand to his chest and peering up at him with solidarity in her every fiber. "I know you're hurting, but wouldn't it help to talk to them? To tell them and *show* them what you're showing me right now?"

Lin hadn't heard anything good about his family, and from what she had sensed from them they weren't the most approachable people, yet it didn't change the fact they'd always have ties to Karl. She was raised differently. She got that. Culturally, children didn't disown their parents—or even elder figures who were *like* parents. As much as she butted heads with her grandfather's mulish personality and narrow perception of the world, she still loved and respected him, and she'd have struggled to envision a world where she didn't need him in her life.

She just wanted to see Karl happy. And she didn't know if making his parents and Cyrus see the pain they had caused him would do that, but she wanted to try whatever would work.

"You're unhappy. Wouldn't talking to them help?"

For a second she believed she'd gotten through to him.

The angry fog reddening his vision cleared, and his brows weren't pinched with the fury he'd been leashing this whole while. But then his face darkened, and she knew she'd lost him even before he stepped back from her and covered his emotions with that impenetrable mask of his.

He turned from her, but not before he grumbled, "I have to go. But you should stay."

Lin watched him alight on the pond's surface with the same ease he'd used to craft his ceramic masterpiece a few days ago. He glided away from her, not looking back once, and when he reached the other side of the ice, he worked quickly to untie his skates and pull them off. Finally, she couldn't look anymore, and she ducked her head, her vision swimming, and her heart paining her awfully.

She'd only wanted to help him, but it seemed she had done more harm than good.

She would've sulked for the rest of the day, but Miranda and Nadine rode over on their ice bikes and encouraged her to join them for some fun. For a while she *did* forget her worries. Eventually, though, it wasn't enough to ignore the memory of Karl's embittered expression. She fretted about him. He was alone someplace and probably believing that no one cared about him.

I care!

She did, and that was why it hurt so much to know he was hurting somewhere without her. Lin had to go to him. It didn't matter if he pushed her away again or shut her out, she had to know that she'd tried.

Getting off the ice, she hurried to unlace her skates.

"Need help with those?" Carrie kneeled to assist before she could protest.

Meekly, Lin admitted, "Karl helped tie them on."

"I noticed." The older woman peeked up at her, a sly twinkle in those sharp eyes of hers. "I also saw and sensed a bit of tension."

She wanted to lie, tell Carrie she'd seen wrong, but she couldn't do it and instead babbled, "He was upset to see his parents and brother, and I tried to cheer him up, but I think he's angry with me now too." She squelched the sob that burned her throat, her eyes watering again, and Carrie's kind face blurring.

Freeing her of her skates first, Carrie sat by her on the bench and draped her arm over her shoulder. Lin turned to her naturally and sunk into the maternal comfort Karl's godmother was offering with no qualms.

"He won't talk to me ever again," she said against Carrie's shoulder.

"Hush. I know my godson, and that's the last thing he'd do."

Lin wanted to seek solace in her words, but her guilt at having pushed Karl to try to make up with his parents was greater. Why had she been so intent? She knew why. She was looking at it through her experience. She'd had her mother walk out on her, and the knowledge had stung for years. Even if she knew that rationally she couldn't have done anything as it had happened when she'd been so young, Lin had still felt *responsible*. Perhaps she hadn't been the easiest child to raise? Maybe she'd driven her mom to the point of no return?

Either way, she didn't love me enough to stay.

And Karl's parents hadn't loved him enough just the way he was.

Lin's heart throbbed painfully for them both. Knowing all that she knew now she had still pushed and pushed and *pushed*—until she'd sent him off to who knew where.

"He hates me," she groused, hopelessly stuck to that belief. "I can't see in what universe he'd want to talk to me again."

"Trust me. He'll do some talking. I've been cooking up this scheme far longer than you've known Karl." Carrie's wicked grin softened after she pulled Lin back by her shoulders and asked her sweetly, "Now, my dear, will you do me the honor of attending a dinner I'll be hosting to-night? I know you missed a couple already, but I don't think you'll want to miss this one."

CHAPTER THIRTEEN

KARL SHOULD HAVE known something was up when Carrie called to ask him over for dinner. He hadn't ever had an unplanned evening at his godmother's. She was nearly as meticulous about time as he was. But he'd put aside his suspicion and give her the benefit of the doubt.

Now he knew he shouldn't have.

His first clue that she had something up her sleeve was that her driveway held two cars he didn't recognize. One a forest-green Jeep and the other a gleaming white Escalade that blended in with the fresh snowfall. He narrowed his eyes at the inconvenience of having to park his truck on the curb.

Carrie's home was one of many older houses in the historic neighborhood overlooking the Bow River and the skyline of downtown Calgary. The home was a charming one-and-a-half-story Craftsman build, its siding painted a mellow blue, and its wide sash windows bordered by bone-white windowpanes. The low-pitched roof sloped over a covered front porch. He stood on that porch and rapped the brass knocker beneath an ornate Christmas wreath, his gaze passing over the holiday lights twinkling from many neighboring homes. Carrie had fully decorated her home as usual. Lights hanging on her rafters spilled over the snow on her front lawn. He knew it was even brighter inside her home.

The door opened and he turned to it—stopping short and losing his ability to breathe for a split second.

Cyrus stood in the doorway. He'd opened the door for Karl, his face plastered with that maddening grin of his. "Hey, little bro." He leaned on the doorjamb and blocked his path. "We have some catching up to do."

As Karl ground his teeth down to nubs, he finally realized what Carrie had been up to…and he didn't like it one bit.

Lin heard the doorbell and knew it had to be Karl.

Everyone else had arrived; he was the only dinner guest that was missing. She'd fretted that he wouldn't show up and wished that she had called him. But after the way they'd left things at the pond yesterday, she didn't think that he'd want to talk to her so soon. It was an irrational thought to think he was upset enough not to speak to her again, but she still worried.

She dried her hands quickly and turned to answer the door.

Cyrus leaped up from his spot on the sofa in the family room and called out, "I'll grab it."

Behind her she felt the comforting press of Carrie's hand on her shoulder. Seeing that she had no choice, she whirled back to continue finishing up in the kitchen with Karl's godmother. At least cooking was keeping her mind off the tense showdown that was likely unfolding in the front entrance between Karl and his older brother.

As she set the dining table, she peeled her ears for any hint as to how it was going with Karl. She didn't know if it was a good thing that she heard nothing other than the low rumble of voices.

Her hands shook lightly as she set cutlery down. Unsurprisingly, she dropped a fork and stooped to pick it up from the earth-toned carpet beneath the dining table. Lin stood and choked a gasp when she saw Karl standing across the table from her. He had the same forbidding scowl in place. Obviously, nothing had changed for him. And he wasn't happy that Carrie had invited his family to dinner as well.

"She invited you too." He said it in a coldly matter-of-fact way that made her flinch.

Clutching the fork she'd have to change out between her suddenly sweaty hands, she gulped and said, "I couldn't refuse Carrie's invitation for the third time."

He didn't smile.

It was awful timing then that Cyrus walked into the dining room and cut a glance at them both. "Looks like I'm interrupting—"

"Absolutely nothing," Karl snapped and stalked in the opposite direction.

A moment later, she heard the front door slam, and she knew he'd left. Lin's eyes stung. She couldn't move either as her vision swam, her chest so tight that her breaths sawed out of her lungs noisily. She wasn't even aware of Cyrus's presence anymore. The dinner itself was meaningless now that Karl had walked out. She'd hoped that it would give him the chance to hash it out with his family. Not forgive them necessarily but move past the hurt he still clearly hauled along everywhere.

A hand brushed her arm, and she looked up, right into Carrie's soft, knowing eyes.

Lin whispered, "He's gone."

Carrie nodded and rubbed her arm soothingly.

Cyrus had vanished, and she would bet Carrie had something to do with it. After a little sob, Lin took herself down the hall to the powder room that Karl's godmother had showed her earlier. Along the way she heard the front door opening again. Looking back hopefully, she deflated when she saw it was Stefon and Karl's father, Charles, strolling in, their dark cheeks ruddier from their walk out in the cold. They didn't look as though they'd seen Karl, their conversation about sports continuing normally.

She dried her eyes, careful not to smudge her makeup and ruin the effort she had made to look good for dinner. The pastel blouse she wore was one of her favorite tops. She'd paired it with palazzo pants and ankle boots. Her fingers clasped the shiny gold charm that Karl had given her, her thumb caressing the warm metal surface, and her eyes burning with the threat of tears once more.

When she left the washroom, it wasn't with an easier heart: she was as burdened as ever before.

"We have to talk."

Lin nearly jumped out of her skin as she turned the corner and dodged running headlong into Karl. He'd come from nowhere. But she forgot all about the near collision at the sight of him. Even his brooding frown was welcome to her right then. Fighting against the tears cresting at her eyes, she squeaked, "You're back!"

"To my questionable judgment," he growled.

She shivered at the sound of it, not knowing if it was from concern or because it was the sexiest sound he could make. She supposed it was a bit of both. Which made her a terrible person.

Now's not the time to drool over him. Focus, girl. Focus!

"Why did you come back, then?"

"There's something I need to say to you."

"Now?" she asked, breathless with anxiety all of a sudden. Her stomach cramped with her rising nerves. What did he want to tell her? And was it anything that would make her worry more than she had for him?

"Dinner," Carrie said behind them, popping into the hallway and looking at them with a mischievous sparkle in her smiling features. "You'll have plenty of time to chat after we've had our meal."

As desperately as Lin wanted to know what Karl had to say, she followed his lead when he nodded at his godmother and turned to walk back into the dining room he'd stormed out of not too long ago.

But not before she heard him whisper back a promise to her, "After dinner, we talk."

Dinner unfolded as normally as Lin hoped it would.

No arguments broke out in the middle of breaking bread. No one lobbed Carrie's delicious mac and cheese at anyone's head. Karl remained in his seat throughout, even if he avoided making eye contact with his parents and brother. There was a moment where her heart felt like it had stopped when Karl ignored Cyrus who was closer and he asked Stefon to pass the salt. Cyrus had curled his lips back into a teasing grin, but one look from Carrie ended whatever he might have said to his brother.

They made it to dessert walking on eggshells but without any incident.

And that was when any quiet truce was blown to smithereens.

It started with Cyrus vaulting out of his seat and striding over to where Karl stood by the festively arrayed fireplace. He leaned on the other side of the mantel and grinned widely at his brother.

"So did Mom and Dad tell you I'm leaving the company?"

Of course he said it loudly and in the already-cozy family room it carried over to everyone's ears. Stefon had been chatting with Charles when the other man went silent and darted narrowed eyes to his coldly statuesque wife. Serenity Sinclair was a gorgeous woman, but she would've looked more approachable if she eased up on her tight-lipped frown. She had looked like she was swallowing something sour all night, and now that look only magnified at what her eldest son had said.

For his part Karl appeared unaffected by

Cyrus's news. Taking a swig of his amber drink, he walked over to a side bar and poured more of the golden liquid from a decanter. His brother shadowed him and filled a glass of his own.

"You know why they're here, don't you? I step down, and naturally they're looking for a replacement." It was obvious what he meant, but Cyrus nudged him. He stopped abruptly when Karl growled low.

"Is that why you've come?" Karl's eyes flashed to his parents.

Lin revised her earlier observation of him being unfazed. She snapped her eyes between the two sides, Karl and his parents, her heart in her throat and her anxiety making her slide down the sofa. She was nonconfrontational by nature. If she'd been anything like Karl, she'd have already started her business long ago and would have had no trouble making her grandfather see that she was perfectly capable of pursuing her own goals and dreams.

But she wasn't, and she didn't care to be caught in the crossfire, no matter how much she wanted to rush over to Karl's side and be supportive of him. This wasn't her battle to help him fight. He had to do this on his own. She just hoped it would free him of his troubling past with his parents.

"Because if it is, I'll stop you right now and

save you the time. I'm not interested in anything that has to do with this family."

"I told you he won't listen," Cyrus said, his tone matching his smug smirk. He drained his tumbler and set it on the mantel, the back of his hand swiping over his mouth, and his swagger full of the kind of trouble that would only increase the friction in the room. "Karl's still hurt that you kicked him out, Mom and Dad."

Lin cringed and sneaked a peek at Stefon. He looked as uncomfortable as she felt.

"It's been a while, though. A long time to hold onto that chip on your shoulder." Cyrus looped his arm around Karl's shoulder and grunted when it was whacked away. He clutched his hand and chuckled. "Guess you're pissed at me too, little brother."

Karl glowered back at Cyrus, but he didn't add fuel to the fire.

Just as Lin thought it might be over, she shrank back in her seat when Serenity sucked her teeth. "Enough. Cyrus, you're embarrassing yourself."

Cyrus scoffed and stroked his beard. It was thick and dark and as wild as his eyes were in that moment. Flexing his bulkier frame, he crossed his arms and looked twice as big as he'd done a moment earlier. Where Karl was lean and tall, his brother was of stockier build. Cyrus had the kind of muscles that could only be developed with a regular weight-resistance regimen. Lin didn't like the odds of him fighting Karl at all. The instinct to protect the man who'd supported her and loved her body so thoroughly was rearing up again.

Before she attempted to defuse the drama, Lin watched as Serenity rose to her feet, her willowy frame in a slinky patterned silk suit. She had her hair elaborately pinned to the back of her head with wispy tendrils curling from her temples. In short, she looked every part the boss that she sounded when she snipped, "Haven't we raised you both with manners?"

Karl bared his teeth. "You barely raised us."

"He has a point," Cyrus piped in.

Charles stood as well and bristled. "Don't talk back to your mother."

"She stopped *being* my mother the instant she kicked me out," Karl snarled, his chest heaving and his glare slicing through his parents. They both looked aghast at the outburst. He'd stunned them into silence.

Lin grimaced and resisted covering her eyes to see what would happen next. It could only get worse from here…

She sighed when Carrie emerged from the kitchen with a tray of cookies and a pot of tea. Lin didn't think she could be more relieved to see Karl's godmother. Carrie took one look around the room, scowled and snapped, "What's going on? You boys better not be thinking of tearing up my home."

"No one's tearing up anything," Charles said emphatically and pinned a strong look at his sons as if they weren't grown men who were beyond parental censuring. "This isn't a polite topic. We'll discuss this privately later."

"No. I'm done talking." Karl regarded Lin, the fury that had painted his features still present in the brackets around his mouth and the steel in his eyes. "I'll wait for you outside."

Awkwardly, she looked around the room and ducked her head, muttering a quick excuse for leaving so quickly before trailing after him. Karl was waiting at the foot of the porch. He looked up, his shoulders and bald head slick from the snow drifting down from the darkened sky. She slipped her coat on and hurried to catch up when he stalked toward his truck. When they were ensconced inside, he gripped the steering wheel, bowed his head, and strained to say, "Give me a second."

She gave him as much time as he needed to regain his composure.

He hadn't been himself at all in there. It was like she'd witnessed a whole new side to him. When she had first met him, Lin had thought he'd just been cold and unfeeling. Then Karl had shown her the gentle, warm side to him by doing a number of kind things for her. More recently she'd discovered he was also the perfect lover.

But now she'd seen him angry, and it had been like an icy fire, a full mix of his hot-and-cold personality. Now he was trying to retrieve the mask he'd lost when he had confronted his family, and Lin wasn't sure she wanted him hiding away.

"Sorry that you had to witness that." He didn't turn his head, but she could tell from his profile that he was still fighting for control of his emotions.

"It wasn't your fault." His brother had been baiting him. Anyone who had been weaker than Karl would have already started a brawl in there. It was commendable that he'd had enough restraint to simply walk out when he had. She had to admit that dinner hadn't panned out the way she or Carrie had hoped. Looking up at his godmother's cozy-looking home, Lin wondered how Carrie and Stefon were faring in there with Karl's parents and Cyrus.

"It is my fault."

Lin snapped her head to him. "How?"

"I should have left when I figured out what Carrie was trying to do."

"What do you think she was trying to do?" She bit her lip nervously. She'd known what was awaiting him, and she had avoided giving him a warning, believing that it would be for the best. She hadn't thought it was *this* bad with his family. Guilt snapped at her heels as she sat frozen, waiting with bated breath to hear what he had to say.

Karl wrung his hands over the wheel. He hadn't started the engine yet. And it didn't seem like he was in a rush to leave anymore. She didn't blame him. It felt like they were trapped in their own little world. The hush around them was peaceful and a far cry from what it had been like inside Carrie's home just then.

"Carrie is caught up in her own happiness. She can't accept that not everyone has to be happy around her."

"Is it a bad thing for her to want you to be happy?"

He drummed his thumbs over the wheel. "I wasn't happy in there. I don't think I ever will be happy near my parents." Expelling a sigh then, he grumbled, "Again, I don't mean to dump my problems in your lap. What happened in there... shouldn't have happened. I'm sorry if it ruined your evening. I'll have to call Carrie and Stefon and apologize later."

Lin's guilt manifested with a lump in her throat that kept her from saying anything.

She could only nod stiffly when Karl asked, sweet again as always, "Want a ride home?"

"Do you want me to walk you up?" Karl looked over at Lin as he pulled to a stop in front of her apartment's entrance. The well-lit foyer kept him from fearing for her safety.

After tonight, he wouldn't be surprised if she refused to see him again.

He had given in to his anger, and the volatile emotion had chewed him up and spit him out. It had been an awful feeling having so little control over himself. His family had brought out the worst in him, as usual. When he'd been young, it had been a helpless feeling, knowing that he had nowhere else to go. For the longest time, and really up to the point they'd kicked him out, Karl had believed what they had said about him not being able to amount to anything without their help. His mom and dad had him relying on them completely. Then they had snipped the umbilical cord and pushed him out of the carefully cultivated world he'd known.

If it hadn't been for Carrie, he didn't know where he would be now—whether his life would be as good as it was now, or whether he would have proven his parents right about accomplishing nothing.

He looked at Lin, realizing most of all that he

might not have met her under any other circumstances.

Still, it didn't change the fact that he probably would be smart to avoid close quarters with his parents and Cyrus. Carrie's final event, the vow renewal itself, was closing in fast, and there would be plenty of room in the big reception hall that he'd booked to keep himself far away from his family.

He couldn't say the same about Lin. It wouldn't be as easy to avoid her.

Particularly when she gazed at him so adorably and softly said, "I would like if you did walk me up."

Karl couldn't refuse her.

It wasn't the longest walk. Before long, they were standing in front of her door, and Lin paused to tap the key code into her apartment. She looked at him curiously. "Back at Carrie's you said you had something to tell me. What was it?"

He hadn't forgotten, but he wasn't sure if the window of opportunity had passed.

Studying her, he realized that he couldn't let it go now that she'd brought it up and that he had to try. It had been weighing on him for a while now. And he was sick and tired of kicking it around his head.

"It's about your work."

"What about it?" She fully turned to him, her eyes rounder, and fear surfacing in her dark irises. "Is something wrong with one of my prints?"

He silently cursed his lack of forethought. Naturally her mind had leaped to the worst-case scenario, and he couldn't fault her when he hadn't given her an indication of what type of news he had for her. She had just imagined it was bad.

But he hoped that what he had to ask her would be met positively.

"I could see us working together on future projects. Some of my clients have shown interest in your pieces, and I can confirm that they'd like to meet and see how you'd incorporate your unique designs into their visions for their parties. Of course, there's no pressure in working out of our headquarters anymore. Remote collaborations would suit as well."

"Karl, that's…"

"A lot to take in," he supplied, nodding. "I know. That's why I wanted to tell you early and let you take your time deciding. The offer is open-ended, and I don't need a response until after New Year's. That's when the first interested client has scheduled an appointment."

"I don't need to think about it. I'd love to work with you. It's just… I'm a little surprised." She smiled slowly past the shock, and then more fully. A heavenly sounding laugh bubbled out of her.

She clapped her hands together before her smiling mouth and shook her head, disbelief flowing off her. "Do you really want to work with me?"

He laughed breathily, relief of his own mingling through his voice. "I wouldn't have asked, otherwise."

Lin tossed her arms around him, taking him by surprise with the embrace.

Even so he still recovered quickly and snaked his arms around her, holding her as close as possible, and wishing with all his thundering heart that he didn't have to let her go. If they worked together, though, he would have to stop seeing her as anything more than a colleague. He'd abused his power already. How would her grandfather ever take her seriously if he thought she'd slept her way to her success?

"Thank you," she whispered into his ear, kissing his cheek.

He turned his head and looked into her eyes. Pulling in, he swore it would be for the last time, right before their mouths touched. As always, the sensual reward was mind-blowingly pleasant. He could've kissed her until they both ran out of air. Just as he was contemplating it, he felt resistance from her.

Baffled and breathless, he let her go.

She pulled back abruptly and brushed her hair away from her face, the butterfly clip no longer doing its job as well as it had before he'd mussed her hair. Lin's eyes had gone back to their widened state.

"What's the matter?" he asked, not liking the panicked look on her face. His stomach hollowed. Maybe she hadn't wanted to kiss him. Perhaps he had read the situation wrong...

"I can't lie to you. I have something to tell you too." Her voice pitched and dropped into a croak at the end, a shy little smile curling her lips, and her eyes lowering and avoiding his own. It didn't give him confidence any more than her words had.

Clamping his jaws together, he set his expression to neutral and steeled himself for whatever she had to say.

"I...knew that Carrie was going to invite you and your parents to dinner." Lin covered her face with her hands and continued. "We were just trying to help you. We thought that maybe you needed a little push to confront them, hash it out, and move on and be happy."

He had been preparing himself for everything but that apparently, because he felt her words strike him like a whip. The pain in his heart was devastating. He stopped himself from clutching his chest and grunting. With gritted teeth, he filtered what she said, heard her genuine regret and knew that he shouldn't feel the angry betrayal that was simmering in him. But he *was* betrayed. And by the one person he wasn't expecting.

Then it struck that this wasn't any different from Isaiah.

His ex-boyfriend hadn't been able to stand Karl's anger toward his parents either. Lin was the same: she had been scheming to change him. Even if her heart had been in the right place, her actions had been invasive and wrong. He didn't need anyone interfering in his life. Not his parents. Not his godmother. And certainly not Lin.

"I'm sorry," she sobbed once, looking up from her hands and reaching out with her fingers. "I didn't want you to feel hurt, but I *did* hurt you."

At least she knew what she'd done. Too bad that he was finally understanding that he'd let this go on too long with her. He liked her and had opened up to her, and all he'd gotten was a broken heart.

In a rough voice, he said, "No, I should apologize. I shouldn't have kissed you."

"I wanted you to!" She wrapped her arms around her middle as though she were warding off the same pain carving out his heart.

Maybe she was. Maybe he had so much more to ask her forgiveness for...

"I told you that my mom walked out on me. Well, I never knew what to feel about it.

I thought I should hate her, but then I didn't know her, and I started to wonder if she had been right to leave. I could have been a difficult child to raise. I might have been too much for her to handle. I didn't realize that I cared what her answer was until I saw you with your parents yesterday. You looked like you were in such pain, and I recognized that pain. I feel it right now." She hugged her arms tighter around herself and sobbed. "I don't want you to hate me."

"I don't hate you," he heard himself say, his voice roughened and raw with emotion.

I could never hate you streaked through his mind.

Because he loved her.

It was so obvious now, he almost wanted to bang his head against the wall.

He was in love with her. Foolishly so, and now…now he was hurting himself by ending whatever they had begun. But it was for the best. Isaiah had been right to walk away from him all those years ago. He had been someone different when he let his parents crawl under his skin. Someone he didn't recognize.

Someone I don't like.

Someone who could hurt Lin, just like he was hurting her right now.

"You do," Lin choked. "I can see it. You're looking at me differently."

He was looking at her like a man in love. A man who knew that he was going to break his own heart just to save her from tying herself to someone who was capable of hurting her.

"I don't hate you, Lin. I…just don't want to do this anymore."

She understood. He knew she did, because she flinched back from him.

Cowardly, he rasped, "We'll talk when we both have had time to think about this. It doesn't change the job offer." He wouldn't take that away from her. She had earned working with his well-heeled clients.

Lin turned her back to him, unlocked her door and looked back, teary-eyed. "I don't want the job anymore. Not with us like this now."

She closed the door in his face, and the fact that he had lost her doubly sank in.

He held back his roar of frustration until he was sitting back in his truck. After all his effort to keep love at bay, it had found him again, made his heart skip and then stopped it dead with the pain of losing the woman he loved. And the only person he had to blame was himself.

CHAPTER FOURTEEN

"HOME SWEET CABIN!"

Miranda flung open the door to their cabin with an enthusiasm Lin wished she could muster. The most she could give was a forced smile as she trailed Miranda inside. As quaint and comfortable as its exterior, the cabin's interior was all rustic wood and country charm. Miranda claimed the bed in the loft and climbed the pine ladder up to the space. That left Lin to check out her bedroom.

She dropped back onto the bed and wished the cedary aroma in the room was enough to sweep her away from her troubled thoughts. Instead, she closed her eyes and forced her mind clear. The technique had worked so far. She felt deceptively unburdened already. At least, she did…and then reality came knocking—literally.

Lin's eyes sprung open, and she sat up on the bed.

Miranda said, "I'm heading out to help with the setup. Did you want to tag along?"

Did she want to risk seeing Karl? would be the better question.

They hadn't spoken for a couple of days. The last thing she'd told him was that she wouldn't work with him. Which was crazy, because his offer had been more than generous—it had made perfect sense for her to accept and have access to his network of clients. But then she'd have to deal with working with him and not being able to be with him…

And it would hurt too much.

She analyzed why it had stung to think that he might be angry with her. For two nights she racked her brain, and she'd only come to one conclusion. She had fallen in love with him accidentally. She hadn't wanted to. It hadn't been a part of her plan. But it had happened, and it would explain why it felt as though her heart had been torn out.

Like it wouldn't ever be healed and whole again.

"Is that your brother?" Nadine stopped midsentence and pointed across the long hall.

They had most of the tables installed for the reception, and the decor was coming together quickly. Red, green and black were the main color choices for Carrie's Kwanzaa-themed vow renewal, but he'd included earthy tones of brown and beige as well to soften the bolder palette. Lin's three-dimensional contributions stood out to him the most. There were also ornate name cards, vases for the floral arrangements, and candelabra that towered over the guests at each table. She had gone above and beyond in a short amount of time, and all on her own.

It would be hard to walk into her studio under his offices and find it empty without her.

But it was expected.

She hadn't ever planned to stay longer, and after how he had left things with her, there wasn't a chance of that changing now.

So seeing Cyrus was the last thing he wanted. One look at his brother and he recalled the events that had led up to him letting Lin go.

"I'll just go over there and continue monitoring the setup," Nadine said, walking off with one last curious look over her shoulder.

He was grateful that she wouldn't be within earshot of what he had to say to his brother. He didn't need one other person looking at him as strangely as Lin had last night.

"Reception is off-limits until tonight." He growled the words, the warning in them implicit.

"Easy." Cyrus tossed up his hands in a placating gesture. "I just wanted to check up on you."

Since when had he and Cyrus been close

enough for his brother to ever want to check up on him? Karl didn't know what he was up to now, but he didn't want any part of it.

"I have work to do."

Cyrus rolled his eyes and flapped a hand at the venue. "I can see that. You're doing a helluva job, by the way." He whistled long and low, his eyes casting over the whole space. All eight thousand square feet of vaulted ceiling and exposed wooden beams, shiny hardwood floor and picturesque views of the Rockies from where the resort stood perched atop a lakeside valley. "If I'd known you were this good, I would have had you throw some of the companies' parties."

Softening him with compliments wouldn't work. Karl stood imperviously in the face of it. "Just tell me what you want and go."

He expected more of a struggle. But Cyrus rubbed his beard with both hands, blew a big breath and said, "Okay. I get it. I'll get out of your hair—uh, well, you know what I mean." He broke off with a laugh and a wave at Karl's bald head.

"Cyrus..." he warned, his anger barely leashed.

"Yeah, anyways, I'll go. I wanted you to give me five minutes—"

"You have them," Karl interjected and he was starting the timer now.

"Fine. Since you're not giving me a whole lot of time, I'll start by saying I'm sorry."

Surely he hadn't heard his brother correctly. Had Cyrus apologized to him just now? If he'd thought he knew what was going on, he wasn't as sure any longer.

"The dinner at Carrie's got a little out of hand." Cyrus snorted and amended, "Actually, it got more than out of hand. I shouldn't have riled Mom and Dad up the way that I did."

"Why did you?" He wasn't about to let the opportunity slip by, no matter how uneasy Cyrus appeared. His brother had tormented him growing up, and all for the sake of pleasing their unpleasant parents. Had it been worth it? Because Karl and his siblings weren't close the way they probably should be. And Cyrus had helped create the rift when they'd all been younger.

"Old habits," his brother said, nervously palming the nape of his neck. He then ran that big hand over the top of his thick afro. "I was a jerk. I still am, but now I'm a jerk with more of a conscience. I realize you have no reason to believe that I'm being genuine right now, but I *am* sorry, Karl. It's part of why I'm here."

Paint him cynical, but he wasn't buying it.

"If you're done," he said while pointedly looking to the exit and hoping that Cyrus got the message.

Instead of arguing and pushing back, Cyrus heaved a big sigh, and his too-broad shoulders sagged. He looked weaker suddenly. "Cool. I appreciate you listening, anyways."

He was walking off when Karl, out of sheer curiosity and *not* sympathy, asked, "Have you really quit?" Soon as he had been able, Cyrus worked his way through the company and eventually sat in the VP of Operations chair at both their parents' companies. He had sacrificed a relationship with his siblings for it, so Karl had always assumed his brother would never have left working for their parents, and that one day he'd inherit the companies for his loyalty.

"I've given them a month to find my replacement. I figure it's the least I could do—not that Mom and Dad are making it easy for me."

That he could see. Their parents had to be seeing red. Cyrus had always been their first choice as the heir apparent, and when it was obvious that none of their other children cut it, they'd put all their eggs in one basket with their eldest son. Of course now Cyrus was leaving, they had no one else to fall back on in the family. Karl might not be close to his sister and younger brothers, but he knew that they'd been like him and fled the clutches of their parents as soon as they possibly could. He couldn't see any of them returning to the fold just to be micro-managed by their parents.

"Why leave now?" he asked.

Cyrus shrugged and hooked his thumbs in the pockets of his faded jeans. "The truth is that we haven't seen eye to eye in a long while, and my leaving the company has become the best thing for me."

"How?" Karl should have been pushing him out the door. He didn't know why he cared why Cyrus was doing whatever he was doing, or what he had planned that had brought that serene smile to his brother's face. It was unlike his usual smugly grinning mug.

He actually looked at peace with his decision to leave their parents.

"I found someone, and she's opened my eyes to how unhappy I've been."

A woman. Of course. It made sense.

Cyrus seemed to read his mind as he shook his head and laughed. "It's not what you're thinking. I'm not ready to marry her, but we've been dating for a few months, and she's just moved to Toronto to open her restaurant."

Why did that sound familiar? He thought of Lin, and his heart throbbed oddly.

"I'm thinking of helping her run it. But it's still early days, and I have job interviews lined up with companies—"

"What do Mom and Dad think of you job-hunting?"

Cyrus snorted laughter and raised an eyebrow. "What do you think? They aren't coping well, let's just say that. I think they thought I'd never move on."

"To be fair, none of us thought you would."

His brother stared at him quietly and unblinkingly for a while, and then he said, "After you left all those years ago—"

"I didn't *choose* to leave," Karl cut in with clenched teeth.

Cyrus nodded, correcting himself. "After Mom and Dad forced you out, I always wondered whether you were happier for it, in the end." He cocked his head, his gaze assessing before he smiled. "You *look* like you're doing all right. Are you?"

If he'd asked him two days ago, before he had proven that he hadn't grown past the scars their parents had left him with, and prior to showing Lin how messed up he was, Karl would easily have said he was doing well for himself. Better than their parents had ever thought he would do. He couldn't answer with the same confidence right now.

And he didn't have to linger to see pity in his brother's eyes.

Nadine returned and she looked pressed for

time. "Sorry to interrupt, but I need your opinion on this."

Karl seized the excuse and turned away from Cyrus. But throughout the day, he returned to their conversation and to the question of whether he was happy or not. And if he wasn't, he had to ask himself what it would take to *be* happy.

Lin walked to the rehearsal dinner on her own from the cabin she shared with Miranda. It was a short distance, but she wished she'd thought better than to wear fancy heels en route. She also wished that she'd invested in a better winter coat, like Karl had told her to do earlier on. Shivering, she hurried along the path through the parking lot into the long log building that would host tomorrow's reception.

She was in such a hurry to get indoors, Lin narrowly missed ramming into someone.

"Karl," she yelped.

His brows vaulted up, genuine surprise breaking up his emotionless mask. "Lin." His voice was deep and soft, and she'd missed hearing it. He looked amazing in his silk black suit. Too good for her to not admire him and suffer her heart's pain a little while longer in his company.

"Am I late?" she asked, looking around at the nearly full room.

"No, grab a seat. We're about to start."

He would've passed her after another curiously long and ponderous look at her, but Lin snagged his arm, and she kept hold of him even when his eyes zipped down to where her fingers alighted on him.

She opened her mouth, thinking that she knew what she wanted to say but blanking on words.

"I should go," he said and slipped free of her hold.

She watched his long, fast strides carry him away from her.

The rehearsal dinner flew by smoothly. Lin glimpsed Karl's parents at one table and Cyrus at another. Carrie must have had something to do with the seating arrangement. Judging by the daggers Karl's parents threw Cyrus's way, she confirmed it had been a good call on Carrie's part. Lin searched for Karl throughout the two-hour event. He had made himself scarce, though. By the time everyone was leaving, she'd given up looking for him.

At least she had, until Carrie stopped her on her way out of the reception hall.

"He's in the kitchen."

Lin was about to head that way, not knowing what she would say, only that she wanted to see him. The only thing that stood in her way was her ringing phone. She was surprised to see her grandfather's name appear on the screen. He hadn't been returning her calls or messages. Now he was calling her out of the blue, and her first thought was concern that something was wrong.

She looked toward the double doors leading into the kitchen longingly, the phone pressed to her ear.

One thing at a time.

Her grandfather first, and then…

Then, she hoped, Karl.

CHAPTER FIFTEEN

CARRIE AND STEFON were glowing with smiles when they were saying their vows to each other the next day. His godmother hadn't ever looked more radiant in a floor-length silver gown that sparkled with crystals embedded in the bodice and long train. Stefon stared at her like a man in love should, and Carrie gazed back with the same answering love.

They spoke their heartfelt promises to each other under a floral arch and, with the still, blue mountain lake behind them, lit six of the seven candles on Lin's specially made *kinara* and faced the riotous ovation from their guests when they turned, with matching smiles, to face them.

Karl clapped and watched from the sidelines, his heart full for them, but his head scrambled by another concern.

Lin had excused herself from the service, the news coming directly from her cabinmate. Apparently she hadn't been feeling well enough to attend the renewal ceremony.

He had thought to apprise Carrie of that fact. He didn't want his godmother thinking Lin had snubbed her, even though he didn't know why that mattered. So he saw to it that Carrie knew, only to have his godmother surprise him by explaining that Lin had dropped by for an early breakfast in the morning and informed her and Stefon on her own. This had unfolded before the ceremony, and he was left fretting through the whole half-hour service about how Lin was feeling right then.

I should go check on her.

Karl was overseeing the caterer, but he pulled Nadine aside and asked her to step in for him. She hadn't complained. In fact, she shot him a knowing look and patted his arm as if she knew *exactly* why he was in such a hurry to leave.

It was the same look that Carrie and Miranda also flung his way as he passed them.

And it was a different look from the scalding glares his parents were lasering from their chairs.

He reached Lin's cabin in record time, but when he knocked, hard enough to rattle the oak door in its frame, he realized that she wasn't in.

Or she's ignoring me.

But he didn't notice the curtains rustling or hear any sounds from inside.

Racking his brain for other ideas as to where to find her, he tried the reception hall. All the finishing touches had been put in the room earlier, and now it awaited the hosts and their guests, but it was devoid of Lin. Frantic now, he searched the trails connecting to a dozen other cabins and didn't run into her. His heart was in his throat by the time he dialed her number shakily.

It rang six torturous times before the call passed to her voice mail.

He followed the instructions of her chirpy prompt and in a strangled voice left her a message. "Call me."

Then, because he didn't like staring at his phone, he texted her too.

Dragging a hand down his face, he swallowed hard and evaluated his behavior. He'd been acting irrationally since he had walked off on her a few days ago. Nothing had felt the same since then. It was a miracle that he'd been able to concentrate and pull off Carrie's event without a hitch. But now that he was almost through working, he didn't have anything else to keep him occupied, and it amplified his desire to find Lin, ensure she was all right, and then…

And then, what?

He had to walk away again, didn't he? That would be the noble thing to do. He couldn't afford to be selfish, not if in the long run he'd be hurt, and she would be hurt, and the love he now knew he had for her transformed into disinterest. Or, worse, *hate*.

He slid his back down a tree and sat crouched on the side of the trail, his eyes glued to his phone, his body ready to wait on her for however long it took for her to get back to him. He just needed to know that she was okay.

Then he swore he'd be okay.

She wasn't all right at all.

Lin had bitten her nails to the quick, nervously waiting on Machelle's call. She sat back in the sleigh and turned her heated cheeks to the wind whipping through her curls. Her hair was probably a mess by now. Two laps in the sleigh and she was looking at a third. Luckily the driver was accommodating and simply shrugged when she paid him for another quick whirl through the wooded trails.

She pulled the woolen blanket that had fallen to her feet up over her legs. It wasn't enough to keep the cold from stinging at her, but it would have to do. She wasn't ready to get off the sleigh. Not until she heard from Machelle about how her grandfather was doing.

Lin was clutching her phone and gazing at it when it rang.

Karl's name confronted her, demanding to be picked up, and she almost gave in, but she stopped herself from tapping on the button to accept the call. What could she say to him? What did he have to say to her? She wasn't ready either way, and it was better to conserve her energy for her grandfather. She hadn't slept since she'd answered his call yesterday and discovered it was her grandfather's new housekeeper who had called to tell her that he'd had a tumble down the stairs. It had been bad enough for him to go to the hospital for immediate surgery.

She had called Machelle, and her friend had dropped everything when she'd heard and gone to check on him. Machelle had promised to call once she had information, but that had been hours ago, and still no call.

All she'd been able to think was that this could've been prevented if she had never left his side. Instead, she'd been selfish and thought only of her own happiness. Now her grandfather was suffering the consequences of her being a bad granddaughter.

This was the thinking that had kept her up all night.

She hadn't slept a wink, and she'd risen early to visit Carrie and excuse herself from what she knew would surely be a lovely celebration. She just didn't have the heart to sit through that touching display when her heart was miles away in an operating room.

Her grandfather was all she had left. She couldn't lose him, and now more than ever with Karl angry at her.

Lin's eyes smarted, and she closed them tight, wiping at the tears that had pinched free.

She slid down the bench and drew the blanket up around her shoulders, her hands still gripping her phone when it buzzed with a message. When she checked, she saw that Karl had not only called but had also left her a voice mail *and* sent a short text.

The text simply read Call me.

The voice message was longer.

"Lin, I heard you're not feeling well. Just call me when you get this. I'm…worried."

She listened to him a couple more times, and it did sound like he was genuinely concerned for her wellbeing. After hearing what had happened to her grandfather, she'd only thought of Karl more and how lonely she was feeling. He was still running through her mind. She hadn't wanted to leave Canada thinking that she had destroyed the relationship they'd had.

She loved him. And it was the first time she'd loved anyone, so she didn't know if she was doing this right, or what words and action would do her feelings for him justice. What she *did* know was she didn't have to be alone.

The horse-drawn sleigh was waiting for him where Lin said it would be.

Karl still had doubts that she'd be waiting for him until he climbed up and saw that she was huddled under a scratchy-looking thick blanket on the other side of the vehicle. Once Karl was ensconced in the sleigh as well, the driver tipped his top hat back at them and signaled for the horses to move. The sleigh rides were available to the guests after the ceremony and all during the reception once it began. He just didn't think anyone had taken opportunity to use it yet. That was why he hadn't gone looking for her there.

Looking her over, he saw the usual healthful color in her cheeks. A little red tinged the tip of her nose, and her lips looked rosier, but her eyes were bright and alert and…perhaps a tad wary of him.

He sighed quietly, realizing that he had a lot of damage to undo.

"I heard you weren't feeling too hot." He frowned when she shivered and noted that she was dressed for the party in a thin-strapped dress. Her coat wasn't buttoned up. And if she wasn't sick, she'd be asking to come down with something miserable soon enough. Without thinking too much on it, he shrugged out of his jacket and draped it over her shoulders. He had to slide over on the bench to do it, and it brought him closer to where her softly floral perfume draped over him. Karl bit down on an appreciative groan. What mattered was that she stopped shivering. Once she did, he breathed easier, and he felt strong enough to control his desire for her from ruining everything as it had before.

If she was leaving him, he wanted closure for them both. The kind that they could eventually move past one day.

Do you want to end things, though?

He packed that thought away. This wasn't about him and what he wanted or even needed.

"I'm not sick in the traditional sense." She gripped his coat and pulled it around her shoulders tighter, her eyes scanning his face, her expression guarded. "What are you doing here?"

"I was concerned." He'd made that obvious, hadn't he?

"That's nice of you. But I'm okay."

Karl didn't know how, but he knew that she was lying. "You're not okay." He didn't care if she got angry. He'd meant it about being worried for her. His unease wouldn't quit until he knew why she looked like she'd been crying. The puffiness around her eyes were a tell. And she sniffed every now and again, and he didn't think she was getting a cold.

Rather than snapping at him to mind his own business, Lin looked away and sniffed again, which made him dead certain that she was crying.

He reached for her and then curled his fingers into a clenched fist that he dropped at the last moment. It killed him to just sit there. The heart that he'd believed irreparably broken had started beating harder and faster, the pressure over his chest intensifying, and the helplessness he felt debilitating. But he knew he'd be doing more harm if he interrupted her now. She had to work through her emotion on her own. He waited quietly until she composed herself, discreetly wiping at her face with a hand, and turning back to him only when she felt ready.

"It's my grandfather. He…slipped and fell down the stairs at home. The housekeeper was home, luckily, and he received care immediately, but—" She choked off at this point and looked away again.

This time Karl sought her hand to give her as much comfort as she was willing to take.

Lin squeezed him back. "He's in surgery, and I'm waiting on Machelle to call with a report."

Now he understood why she'd left. It all made sense. He was conflicted. In a sense, he was happy that *she* was feeling well, but he knew just how close she was to her grandfather, and it must have been eating away at her to know that she was thousands of miles away from her family and friends and everything she knew and loved because he'd given her a chance to work with him.

It's my fault she's feeling this way right now.

"I don't know what I'll do if he…if he…" She sniffed a few more times, and her shoulders shuddered with silent sobs.

Deciding to let instinct reign, he pulled her into his chest and felt easier with her head buried against him and her tears pressed into him. She cried for a while, and he soothed her as best as he could, quietly stroking her soft, honey-colored hair. The driver was slowing as they neared the end of their circuit, but a quick jut of his chin cued him to continue pulling through another short lap. All around them, looped through bare black branches, were thousands of strung lights. Their multicolored glow brightened as the storm clouds gathered and thick, fat snowflakes began swirling from the sky. A concealed sound system played slow Christmassy jazz, and the holograms of a group of cheery carolers that he'd had installed for the sleigh ride waved at them as they passed. It might have been romantic, but all he cared about was the woman in his arms.

Lin cried through all of it, her sorrow muffled into him.

She was breaking his heart. He didn't know how to help her. All the money in the world couldn't magically take her sadness away. Not that she needed his money; he just wanted to help. Desperately. Maddeningly so.

He gauged the time by the density of snow-flakes that had come to rest on the driver's top hat.

By the time Lin pushed off his chest and looked up at him, the driver had a thick brim-ful of snow.

"I soaked your shirt." She trailed her fingers over the wetness that now adorned his shirt-front. Face crumpling, she appeared on the verge of crying once more.

"It's fine," he murmured soothingly.

She shook her head, but he ignored her pro-test and held her. Lin allowed him, her tears sparser now. The next time she lifted her head, she had a watery smile for him. She wiped at her face and laughed hoarsely. "I'll have to fix my makeup," she groused.

"You look beautiful." He wasn't gassing her up either. She would always look gorgeous to him.

The sleigh had long stopped, and he hadn't

asked the driver to continue. Instead, Karl coaxed Lin out and guided her down the trail that would take her back to her cabin. As they walked, he sensed she wanted to say something when she squeezed his hand.

"Thanks for caring enough to find me."

"You'd have done the same for me, I'm sure," he replied.

"You should go back to the reception. It should be starting right now. Carrie will want you there."

He seriously doubted Carrie would want him to abandon Lin in her time of need. He didn't say this to her, of course. "I'm not missing anything. I'll pop back in when I know you've heard from your friend."

"What if...what if it takes all night?"

"I'll stay with you for however long it takes."

It was the relief, subtle and sweet, on Lin's face that made him realize he'd said the right thing and made the right choice.

Lin hadn't thought Karl would actually stay with her as he said he would. She wouldn't have been cross with him either if he'd had to leave. His godmother's big party was happening, and she was keeping him from celebrating with everyone. Lin's guilt had been real and ugly in the first hour. She'd tried to get him to go, even though it was the very last thing she wanted at the moment.

But each and every time Karl rebuffed her suggestions for him to leave.

He made himself cozy in her shared cabin. At one point he made hot chocolate for them to drink before the woodstove.

Maybe it was the belly full of warmed cocoa, or the heat of the fire when the snow only thickened and fell faster outside...

Or maybe I like the way Karl's sitting so close.

His arm tossed casually over the back of the sofa they were leaning against, and his fingers brushed her shoulder every so often, the brief caress setting off a dizzying need through her. She hadn't forgotten why they were sitting there, isolated in a cabin, just the two of them—but it was also hard to erase the memories of how good it had been with him.

How good he was for her.

Her head slumped forward, eyes drifting shut. She jerked them open and snapped her head back. But a second later she was doing it again. Listing to the side and then catching herself before she leaned against him. Her head had just touched his shoulder when she backed away quickly, muttering an embarrassed apology.

When it happened yet again, Karl simply curled his hand around the back of her neck and held her to him. "Sleep," he instructed in that bossy way of his.

Lin blushed profusely, but sure enough, her eyes closed, and she slipped into a dreamless sleep.

She didn't know how long she slept, only that when she awoke, it was to the discovery that night had fallen, the snow brighter and illuminating the interior of the cabin. She saw that she'd been lying half-sprawled over Karl, her head on his chest, her hand over his heart, and one of her legs resting atop both of his. He had stuffed a sofa cushion behind his head, and she felt a little better knowing he hadn't completely sacrificed his comfort to see to hers. She was careful in moving up to stare at his peaceful face as he slumbered. It was a rare moment when he wasn't actively masking his emotions.

Lin studied him for a long while. By the time she had to pull away to go to the bathroom, she was confident she could count the number of his eyelashes.

Karl was awake and sitting up when she'd finished freshening up.

He had her phone in his hand. "Your friend called. I told her you'd call right back."

Lin could have kissed him. It wasn't a call she'd have wanted to miss. She took the phone and saw that he was standing to leave, likely wanting to give her some privacy. She grabbed hold of his hand as he passed her.

He looked down to where she was sitting, staring up at him, half his face shrouded in shadow, the other half in the dying embers' light from the stove.

"Stay," she begged.

Karl stared hard at his and Lin's interlaced fingers. He concentrated on their hands while he listened to her one-sided conversation with her friend. He couldn't make out anything that was being said, and she wore a good poker face, except when she gasped and squeezed his hand tightly near the end.

He stroked his thumb over the back of her hand, willing his strength into her.

When she finally ended the call, he was on pins and needles for the news, and it took all his willpower to keep from rushing her to tell him what she'd been told.

Lin didn't leave him in suspense. "He's going to be all right." The smile that glowed through the whole of her face wiped clear all his worries on the matter. Lin went on to explain that her grandfather had had surgery to fix a hip fracture and that he'd need to recover for a while. Her friend had already offered to move in temporarily, and the hospital was also sending a nurse home with him for the first week. Long enough until Lin could get home and take over his care.

She collapsed into his open arms by the end of it, her eyes watering, and her sniffles back in full force.

He hugged her closely and whispered soothing words to her. She'd handled herself well, given how concerned she'd been for her grandfather. Meanwhile, he'd been concerned out of his mind for her. Now he could rest easy knowing that she would spend her last few days in Canada with a lighter heart before she left for her home where she would help her grandfather recover.

Not wanting to think about her departure, he tucked her into an embrace.

The sound of fireworks was what pulled them apart.

"Is that what I think it is?" Lin wiped at her eyes.

"Yes, they were a surprise for Carrie. A little early until we start counting down to the New Year, but would you like to go watch the show with me?"

They walked out of her cabin, hand in hand, in search of the fireworks. They had just cleared the snaking forest trail when they saw the first burst of pyrotechnics light up the sky in a wash of gold, purple and red. Lin gasped when another went off, this one bright enough to illuminate the forest and the lake. He had to admit that it was quite a sight, a stark contrast to the shadowed mountains in the background with the colorful light display entertaining them much closer.

He spied a few people coming out of the forest. Other guests who weren't part of Carrie's party but who were there to enjoy the fireworks he'd had prepared for his godmother on her special day.

Looking down at Lin, he wondered what he'd do without her. He couldn't remember what his life was like before she came into it.

She glanced up and caught him staring, her eyes reflecting some of the electric colors of the fireworks. Her mouth moved, but he couldn't catch anything over the explosive noise of the fireworks.

Lowering his head, he leveled his ear closer to those glossy, tempting lips of hers.

"Are you still upset with me?" she implored.

She would think that, after he had exhausted his energy avoiding her for the past few days. But he knew that it wasn't because he was angry with her. On the contrary, he knew that he loved her, and it was alarming and exciting all at once. He just didn't want to hurt her. Didn't want this to end badly, as it had with Isaiah. His parents had once again shown him how damaged they'd made him. He wasn't sure whether to thank them for saving Lin from him—or whether he should hate them anew for taking yet another chance at happiness from him.

"I'm not angry," he said firmly.

As soon as the words were out of his mouth, Lin hugged him. It was her lips touching his that shocked him. He'd have melted into her if he didn't feel her moving away already. Too soon for his liking.

Fresh tears shone in her eyes.

God, he'd made her cry again. Before he could thumb away the tears that trailed down her cheeks, she kissed him again. A saltiness flavored her mouth, but he found himself pushing back against her, strengthening the friction of their kiss. This time it lasted long enough for his lungs to burn by the time they pulled back from each other.

"I like you a lot, Karl. I… I just want you to know. You don't have to do anything about it."

His ears were ringing, and he couldn't fault the fireworks or their breathlessly passionate kiss. Still, he heard her clear as day.

She liked him.

And he loved her.

Most of all she wasn't trying to push him to act on what she'd said. True to her word, she gazed up at the fireworks, with a contented smile on her face, those tears still glistening in her eyes.

And then it clicked.

He was standing in his own way. He hadn't been able to save his relationship with Isaiah, but it didn't have to be like that with Lin now. Even as hope unfurled through him, he felt a hiccup of hesitation to act on this new and sudden drive to be with her.

To be *happy*, as Lin had put it a few nights ago.

"I like you too."

He knew she hadn't heard him when a particularly loud crack from the fireworks drowned out his confession. So he did the next best thing that ensured she understood him. He slipped his arm around her and swept her up into another kiss, breaking off quickly to murmur "I like you" against her mouth. She heard him now, her fingers clawing into his shirt, and her round eyes flitting over his face, possibly scouring it for signs that he was joking with her.

Her eyes begged for an explanation.

"It's true. I've been fighting it this whole time, thinking that it would be better if you didn't get caught up in my mess. I'm not…easy to be around. I get that." He'd put his foot in his mouth a few times around her. In fact, it was how their relationship had begun, with him accusing her of stealing her own vase. Now she'd stolen his heart—

No. He'd given it to her freely, just unexpectedly.

"That's why I could never be upset with you. I like you too much."

She smiled slow and shyly, and he felt it because their lips were touching again.

"I need you to know that I'm willing to do anything to keep you with me, as long as you'll allow me."

"I have to go back home," she started.

"I know," he rasped out. "I can wait. Do long distance. I'm open to it." Losing her without putting in an effort wasn't an option. It would be far worse than risking heartache again.

"You'll wait for me," she repeated.

He nodded solemnly.

She draped her arms over his shoulders then, her hands massaging the back of his head, fingers teasing his crown. With another smile, she nodded too. "It's all I wanted. Well, that and *this*."

Lin kissed him, showing him exactly what else she desired besides being with him too.

EPILOGUE

Five months later

LIN WALKED DOWN the stairs of her second-floor studio and through the floor space below that she'd leased and converted into a shop to sell her three-dimensional designs. It was still early in the morning and a good two hours before she opened the doors for business, but she was there because the alarm had gone off. It had sounded briefly before she heard the telltale noises of someone punching in her code to silence the tripped security system.

She clutched the vase in her hand and walked around the corner into the store, preparing to clobber the intruder.

Lin shrieked when she ran into whoever it was and they caught *her* by surprise.

"Lin." Her name came out huskily in a voice she'd recognize anywhere.

She gawked up at her boyfriend. Karl took the

vase from her suddenly nerveless fingers as a little hysterical giggle emerged from her. Her reaction was understandable: she'd nearly sent him to the hospital or the hereafter. A second later and she might have bashed his head in, so she was shaken up a little.

Well, that and she hadn't been expecting to see him for another week. He'd booked off time to visit her as soon as his schedule permitted. He would've flown out sooner, but she had insisted that he focus on his business first. Just because they were dating didn't mean they had to sacrifice their other passions for their new-found love.

Setting aside the vase, Karl tugged her into an embrace that had her relaxing against him.

"I almost knocked you out," she pointed out.

His chuckle drifted through the shop. "Yeah, I saw that."

"I could've killed you." She glared up at him, but it was hard to maintain her annoyance when he pecked her lips and smirked.

"It would've been worth it just to see you."

She rolled her eyes and fought a smile. "What are you doing here? I thought you said next week. Also, you know there's a law about breaking and entering. Someone once mentioned it to me…"

His eyes twinkled at the shared memory.

Their first meeting at Machelle's wedding venue felt like so long ago now. Lin would never have imagined they would be standing here, in her shop, his arms enveloping her, and his mouth descending down to hers.

She moaned around his kiss, a protest bubbling out and dying swiftly as his tongue swept hers up in a tangle.

By the time the kiss ended, she was breathless and blushing in full force. Especially when her phone sang out from the back pocket of her designer jeans. She answered without checking the caller ID and regretted it when her grandfather's voice came through the other end. She sounded out of breath, and he immediately noted it. With a heated face, she stammered through an excuse as to why she sounded like she'd run up and down the stairs, and she swatted Karl's chest when he laughed low. The last thing she wanted was her grandfather putting two and two together. He'd known about her dating Karl, and he had been asking to meet him more formally, but neither of them was expecting her boyfriend to arrive earlier than planned.

Once she was off the call, she yelped as Karl tugged her up against him again and stole a kiss while she was recovering.

"We should have dinner tonight. You, me and your grandfather."

"I don't think you know what you're getting yourself into. He's prepared to interrogate you."

"I survived my parents. Your grandfather should be far easier."

Unlike Cyrus, whom he had started to talk to along with his other siblings, Karl hadn't seen or spoken to his parents since Carrie's big event. It was better that way. He'd faced them and come out stronger for it. Just like she'd finally returned home and gotten her grandfather to accept that she didn't want to inherit his company. It had taken some work, and he was still skeptical, but contrary to her belief, he hadn't cut ties with her the way Karl's parents had. She'd been so convinced that she would lose her only family she didn't realize that she'd gained someone special along the way. Karl…but also his godmother and Miranda and Nadine—all three women kept in touch with her regularly, and Lin was making her own plans to visit Canada again soon.

For now, Karl had come to see her on her home turf.

"Are you going to give me a tour? Or do you want to kiss some more?" He nibbled her lobe and dropped his head to do the same to her throat.

"Stop," she said and giggled but didn't try to push him away.

Eventually he lifted his head and gestured for her to show him around the shop. She complied, weak-kneed from the hickey he no doubt had given her. A love bite she'd have to mask with makeup before she saw her grandfather again.

He kept his hand looped around her the whole while. She pointed out the gold jewelry pieces she'd recently put up for sale. He was not surprised when she told him that the new pieces had been flying off the shelf.

With a knowing smile, he said, "Sounds like you've hit your stride."

She could say more than that. She was already ahead of her rent for the new space, and she'd used the extra revenue to buy another printer to help speed up production and stock. Her 3D designs were unique and coveted, and they might not stay like that forever, but she had plenty of time and drive to revitalize her business and keep it fresh for her customers.

"I see you were inspired," he said, pointing out African charm necklaces and bracelets and then glancing at the necklace he'd gifted her hanging around her neck.

"You could say that." She winked and tugged him along to finish the tour.

And when it was done, she prepared to open up shop. He insisted on staying with her while she worked, and she couldn't bring herself to shoo him out. Mostly because he kept to himself and, if anything, helped by bagging customers' purchases and wiping clean the glass displays. Karl was not only a model boyfriend but the perfect employee.

He stayed throughout the day, except for when he left for a moment but returned with lunch for them, for which she closed shop midday. Then she worked for another few hours before the last of her customers were rung through and she closed up after them. She'd usually finish up for the day by balancing the till, but she knew that she couldn't let Karl stand around any longer than he had already.

"Let's go," she said, grabbing her purse and swinging it over her shoulder.

He took her hand. "Are you sure? I don't mind sticking around longer."

"You've done enough for me. I just want to spend this first night with you *not* working."

They walked hand in hand out of her darkened shop and studio, and she was reminded of the night on New Year's Eve when they had both confessed to liking each other.

She jogged his memory and watched as a smile swept his face.

"I don't like you anymore," he told her, stopping, tucking her closer to his side and tipping up her chin. "Nowhere near as much as I love you."

Her chin trembled, and her responding smile felt wobbly. "I love you too." And she believed she always would.

* * * * *

If you enjoyed this story, check out these other great reads from Hana Sheik

Second Chance to Wear His Ring
Temptation in Istanbul

Available now!